As It Was
ON PA'S FARM

Mary Farley Willis

Pacific Press Publishing Association
Mountain View, California
Oshawa, Ontario

Dedicated

to my husband, Harlum, whose tales of adventure have brought about this book. To our son Pat, his wife, Linda, and their children, Kim and Chris.

Cover illustration by Fred Irvin
Book design by Lauren Smith

Copyright 1980 by
Pacific Press Publishing Association
Litho in United States of America
All Rights Reserved

Library of Congress Catalog Card No. 79-90024
ISBN 0-8163-0393-2

Foreword

Some time ago Mary Farley Willis penned her heart and soul into a manuscript which she dreamed would one day inspire others.

Teaching school and raising a family took precedence over all else, and her dream lay in a chest—not forgotten, just on hold; but inspiring no one.

Inspiration, though, can come from any direction, and a while back Mary was encouraged by her good friend Dr. Ira M. Gish, himself a writer, and author of *Madison, God's Beautiful Farm*, to get her manuscript published. With that encouragement and a lot of prayerful dedication, Mary set to work polishing and finishing her manuscript.

The result is *As It Was on Pa's Farm*, and it is a rare privilege to be able to recommend it to you without reservation. The author is herself a unique Christian woman, deeply dedicated to humanity, with a golden gift for understanding her fellow-men and an Old-South charm that is rare and beautiful.

In this book the author has used her own ability to understand human situations, to share with the reader moments of pure pleasure.

I have had the pleasure and privilege of working with Mary F. Willis in the publishing of her *Women of the Bible* series, and I have found her to be a unique blend of southern belle and modern woman. She tolerates change, and with the same open-mindedness she loves people. She is a Bible scholar and a learned teacher, highly regarded in her community for her integrity and self-discipline. She has invested her talents wisely in the writing of *As It Was on Pa's Farm*.

R. M. "Bob" Tucker
Publisher, *Chilton County News*
Clanton, Alabama

Toby's Sickness

Tom and Valinda Malcolm had been picking cotton since early morning, taking very little time to rest, for the bolls were already popping open and some were falling to the ground. Although fall had come, the days were still hot. If the farmers did not get the crops gathered and taken to the cotton gin before the fall rains set in, the price would drop. The Malcolms needed the highest price they could get, and even that would hardly be enough to meet expenses. Eight years of married life had brought heavy responsibilities to Tom and Valinda Malcolm.

For a moment Valinda stopped working. She wiped the back of her hand across her brow. Beads of perspiration stood out in the crease lines of her forehead. "What're we gonna do, Pa? Toby's sure not well 'n' I don't know what's the matter."

"Do you think he is really serious, Ma? Do you think Toby—is—is?" Tom stammered, showing his concern. He stopped picking the cotton and straightened up.

"I know he's still sick, Pa. I know he's serious sick. But I don't know what's his trouble." Valinda Malcolm began to scratch the sand at her feet with a stick. After a while she spoke again: "The doctor's not helpin' none—not none. What'll we do?"

"Maybe he'll grow out of it. He's only four years old. He'll be fine, Ma." Pa smiled and began to work again.

His wife shook her head. "His little leg is so stiff. It don't get no better. No one around here seems to know anything about what to do. I hate leavin' him alone at the house with only Hank to watch him. Hank's only three, a baby himself; but we can't keep Susan out of school." Valinda sighed, wiped her brow once more, and set to work. "We sure gotta save this cotton crop."

Tom worked steadily and only grunted an affirmative reply to Valinda's statement.

"I don't really think Dr. Hosea's doin' anything to bring about any improvement in Toby." Valinda spoke again as she worked mechanically. She couldn't shake the feeling that little Toby would be lame the rest of his life. "I wish't we could take him over to Benston. But that'd take hours to go there." Valinda knew also that Tom would not want to hurt Dr. Hosea by taking the boy to another doctor. Dr. Hosea was more than just the family doctor. He was a close friend. She knew too that the cotton had to be picked so that they might pay off a debt with the proceeds. Valinda felt sure that Tom did not sense the seriousness of the child's illness.

"You know, Valindy," Pa spoke up, and his voice sounded a little touchy, "Doc's lived here all his life. Fact is, he was borned right here in Oak Valley, hisself, and his pa doctored here even before him."

Ma interrupted Pa. "True, he was borned not more'n a mile from here. And, since that young doctor growed up, he heerd the first cry of every young un under six years old—all in Oak Valley, Maple Hill, and Piney, and all the communities around Larsen—and Larsen to boot. But, jest 'cause he's lived here and's doctored 'em all, well, that don't mean he's a-helpin' Toby none." Ma stopped work for a moment again and straightened her back before she continued. "In Benston they's two doctors. Maybe they know more'n Dr. Hosea does."

Pa kept on picking cotton. Ma noticed the frown on his face when he replied, "Can't we wait a few more days, Ma? Can't we give Dr. Hosea a little more time?"

A loud squeal from the two boys on the porch of the Malcolm home nearby interrupted the conversation. Pa and Ma looked in that direction. The humble home, with the children playing about, was no ill picture. Tom himself had laid the logs in the building—Valinda helping him. They had built the old mud-and-rock chimney that added coziness to the scene. The children, though Toby was not well, appeared happy and content. The two boys seemed carefree, playing together on the porch.

The feeling that she was being unusually impatient about Toby made Ma have a sense of guilt. "I—I—well, I reckon I am too anxious, Pa," Valinda apologized. "But we can't do fer 'em what we ought to do." Then tears came. She bent to her work again.

Pa moved a little nearer to the one who had stood by his side so faithfully through their trying years. He put a rough, suntanned hand on her shoulder in an attempt to comfort her. "We're gonna be all right," he said. "I know we are. It does look hard now. But some day we can do more than we're doin' right now." The words were a poor attempt at a solution to Toby's condition, but he went on: "Maybe Toby'll be all right if we give the doctor time."

His wife wiped her tears on the sleeve of her dress and tried to be brave. Tom could make everything right, it seemed to her.

"We're gonna be all right," Ma heard her companion repeating. "And you know, we will pay the last note to Henry this fall when the cotton's sold."

At the sound of Henry's name something welled up inside of Valinda Malcolm, a feeling of resentment hard to control. That name brought to her mind some unpleasant events of the recent past. Tom Malcolm's father had not been a wealthy man, nor would one have called him poor. Before Valinda and Tom were married, Tom had known what it was to have more than enough. As a young man at home he had worked for his father, expecting to get his share of the inheritance when he married. But it had not worked out that way. His brother Henry, by fraud and trickery, had managed to get all their father's property when the elder Malcolm had suddenly died. So, when Tom and Valinda married, they found it necessary to borrow from Henry to buy themselves a farm. And they were still paying on that unfair debt.

"Pay Henry the note we owe him, indeed!" Those words seemed bitter to Valinda Malcolm. And she expressed the words aloud. "Pay Henry what we owe him!" She raised her voice a little as she spoke. "I—I—" but suddenly she hushed.

"I know what you're thinkin', Ma," her husband said. "I know you can't help feelin' that way about Henry."

"Tom," Ma addressed the man she respected greatly, "you know I don't mean to behave like this. God, forgive me." She always said that when she felt this way about Henry. "And forgive Henry too," she prayed.

"Come on, Ma," Pa urged. "Let's set in the shade by the sassafras bushes and rest a spell. I declare we both need a rest."

Before Tom and Valinda got up from their rest in the shade that the sassafras bushes so graciously lent them, Ma had another idea—a sudden one—all her own. She had seen little Hank chasing after something, a butterfly, no doubt, and he had run to the opposite end of the house, where the eyes of the anxious mother had followed him to the row of trees that lined the trail to the spring in the hollow beyond the house. How cool and refreshing that spring water would be! How good it would feel to tired, aching feet! And then *the* thought had come to her.

"I don't know if it'll help any," Valinda said quietly, "but I don't believe it would hurt none, either. If you'll help me, we'll take Toby down to the spring and dip his legs in the barrel of water. It's been settin' in the sun and should be plenty warm."

The look on Tom's face disheartened her; nevertheless, she went on, "I want to make a try—I want to give it a chance, and I want to go do it now before the day wears on."

"But that water's been settin' there since we set the late potato draws," Pa objected. The barrel was always used for hauling water for newly set out plants; then water was left standing in the barrel to keep the staves from shrinking and falling apart. "Wouldn't you ruther have fresh water?" Pa asked. "The spring's still flowin' and water's a-plenty."

"I know the water's been there a long time, but the fresh water'd be cold, and I want to do this now. That water's warm, and's all right for the first time. Tomorrow morning we can put in fresh water to warm up durin' the day—if this don't make 'im worse."

"But Dr. Hosea might not approve," Pa argued.

"The doctor ain't helpin' none," Ma stated for the dozenth time.

Since Ma seemed bent on doing something in an effort to help their child, Pa began to agree to go along with her, skeptical though he seemed to be. " 'Course," he admitted, "Toby ain't gettin' no better under Dr. Hosea's treatment. Maybe 'twon't do no harm." Then Tom rose to his feet.

When Ma saw that Pa was going to go along with her, she got up quickly herself, and left the half-filled sack of cotton on the ground. Why she felt this way about that notion, she did not know; but somehow she had a feeling that something was about to happen to help the child who was the object of their present concern. She and Pa hurried to the house. Ma reached the children a little before Pa did. With her heart light now, her steps were not so heavy, tired though she was.

The children had grown tired of play, and three-year-old Hank was trying to help his brother get a drink of water. Hank poured the water into a glass from the gourd dipper that Ma had left in a bucket.

"Yer pa and me's gonna give you a treatment, Toby," his mother said.

"Ugh!" was the response the little one made. His face showed his dislike for more medicine. Certainly he let his mother know he remembered every spoonful of medicine he had swallowed.

"Oh, it's not gonna be medicine," Ma hurried to say.

"We're gonna take you swimmin'." Pa tried to help.

Toby handed his half-empty glass to Hank and looked surprised.

Hank set the glass on the water shelf. "Me too?" he asked enthusiastically.

"Yes, you too," Pa promised.

Valinda Malcolm noticed the happy smiles that played on the faces of her youngsters. Hank danced off the porch with delight showing in his grin, but Toby had to be helped.

"You mean we're going swimmin' right now?" Hank asked. It was quite unusual that Ma and Pa could take time to spend with them during cotton-picking time.

Down at the spring, Pa lifted Toby up so that he could put his legs in the barrel of warm water. He began to kick with his good foot and tried to kick with the other one. Hank wanted his turn, but because Ma was afraid to have him in the water where Toby had been and she wanted Toby to spend much time in the water, she found another way to entertain Hank. Although the stream was hardly deep enough to cover his chubby little feet, she helped the little fellow to wade in the stream that flowed from the spring.

For the first day or so no signs of improvement were seen in Toby; but since there were no indications of harm, Tom and Valinda continued the bit of fun and treatment the middle of each afternoon. After all, this venture allowed a rest for the two aching backs of the parents—backs aching from bending over the stalks of cotton so that they might gather and save the white "gold" that would bring the money so much needed.

Dr. Hosea's Visit

For five days Ma and Pa had been giving Toby the water treatments. Now, exhausted from her labors she overslept one morning. Pa had already milked the cow and was making a fire in the cookstove when she awoke with a start upon hearing the poker drop to the floor. Maybe Pa had purposely let the poker drop when he was shaking down the ashes in the cookstove.

Quickly Valinda Malcolm slipped out of the comforts of the bed, got into her clothes, and combed her hair. She went by to take a peek at Toby, almost fearing to look lest he might be worse. Although she had not yet seen signs of ill from the treatments, she was afraid something bad might yet develop. Pa had promised he would not tell the doctor for a while. Ma was afraid Dr. Hosea would have objections and tell them not to put the boy's leg in water at all. Since she was determined to try this simple treatment, she did not want the doctor to know about it yet.

Ma tiptoed, trying not to wake Toby; but he was already awake. Hearing his mother's footsteps, he half sat up in the bed to watch her as she came to his door. He was mischievously grinning at her when she looked in. Ma moved toward the child's bed to feel his forehead for fever. When she did, she thought she noticed something—something that she had hoped for. She looked again. Could it be? The child's foot moved! She knew she saw it.

"Pa!" Valinda yelled, frightening the child with the suddenness of her call. "Pa, come here quick!" Ma paled. Had she been seeing right? Taking the child's foot in her hand, she tenderly squeezed it and told him to wiggle his toes. Pa, standing beside her now, watched Toby try, but with very little sign of movement this time. However, since Ma had seen the sign the one time, she and Pa showed their happiness.

When Susan went off to school and the rest of the morning chores had been tended to, Ma placed the quilt pallet in its usual place on the porch for Toby and did what she could to make things comfortable for the two boys while she and Pa would be in the field. The work went easier that morning. It seemed the cotton filled their sacks faster, and their hearts were not nearly as heavy now. Yet, common knowledge told them danger might not be past. Maybe their treatment had not been sufficiently proven. Although they had a good bit of hope, they were not yet assured, of course.

"It won't be so hard to do without needy things," Ma suggested, when they were picking along the seemingly never-ending rows, "if only Toby can be spared," she sighed. Then, at noon, as the two walked unevenly across the bumpy rows and furrows toward the house, Ma expressed again her always-present thought, "I do so hope we won't have to—to lose him."

Pa squeezed Ma's hand with his own that was too tired to make a very hard impression. He had begun to admit with Ma that it was possible that they might lose their child, although at the first Pa had not really shown signs of taking the matter seriously.

A bit of cloud passed across the sun, and they both blew out a deep breath, smiling their welcome for the comfort the cloud had brought. A breeze caused Ma to remove her sunbonnet so that she might have the full benefit of the refreshing coolness it offered. Pa took off his broad-brimmed straw hat and fanned them both a little.

A few more steps brought them to the edge of the yard. Valinda did not take notice of the clean-swept, bare yard and the beautiful blooming zinnias at the outer edge. As for the yard, it would have been unusual had it been other than clean. Ma kept it that way, with Susan's help. Only had it been otherwise would she have noticed. As for the multicolored blooms on her zinnia plants, she would have taken a few seconds to admire them, but she wished to hurry to check on Toby's condition.

Finding Toby still in an evidently improving state, and both children as hungry as she and Pa were, Ma hurried into the kitchen. She built a fire in the cookstove while her husband did some feeding at the barn. The crackle of the hickory wood had a musical sound today because Ma's heart was somewhat lighter than it had been for some time.

In her haste Mrs. Malcolm had not heard when Tom returned from the barn, nor had she noticed the clop, clop of horses' hooves coming down the country road, bringing a visitor just at mealtime. But when she raised the lid from the black kettle to test the food in it, and tempting odors escaped to float on the air to the outside, she heard an exclamation on the front porch that made her know Dr. Hosea was there.

"Woman, that smells mighty good," came the doctor's words.

"Oh, Dr. Hosea!" Valinda called. She was about to tell the doctor the hopeful news about Toby and her treatment. But, on second thought, she finished with "It's mighty good to have you come by. Do stay and eat a bite with us. Dinner'll be ready in no time."

Pa did not say a thing about Toby. He had promised Valinda he would not. That was his wife's secret, and he would not betray her.

"Good of you to ask me," the doctor said, not admitting that he had actually stopped for that purpose, though Mrs. Malcolm knew full well that he had. "I've been up the road to see Aunt Molly Hinds and just thought I'd stop by and see my favorite little patient here." The doctor turned his eyes to look at Toby, who was having a tussle on the pallet with his roly-poly brother. "I had not expected to find him doing this well," the doctor commented. "Actually I had—well, I had not expected to find him doing—doing—this well," the doctor repeated, fumbling for words to say. For, surely the doctor could not say that he had no hopes of Toby's ever recovering.

After the good food had been enjoyed by all, Dr. Hosea made ready to leave. He thanked Valinda heartily and advised, "Keep giving Toby the medicine I left for him." He looked again at his patient, in evident surprise, and added, "It's certainly good to see him making improvement."

In spite of the doctor's advice, Toby's mother secretly had no intention of giving the little one another drop of the ill-tasting stuff that could not possibly have been helping him anyway. She would tell the doctor later—maybe.

As the days went by, Toby improved rapidly until Ma even dared take him to the field where he might be nearer them as she and Pa worked. He could lie on his pallet in the shade, or even sit up when he felt like it. Actually, he could get about some now. Hank could run about and not feel bound with the job of being nurse for his sick brother. The days were getting somewhat cooler. This made it easier for Toby and Hank to be in the field.

Little Hank was like a bird out of a cage the first day the children were allowed to go to the field with Pa and Ma. He ran from Toby to them, and then from them to Toby. He would run off some distance in search of any interest he might find around. Sometimes he would pick some of the pretty white bolls and poke them into one of the sacks while he listened to the conversation between the older ones.

"I hope to get off another bale this week," Tom told his wife. "That's about all we can expect this year."

"We'll have to get Toby some shoes soon since the weather will be getting cold. I'm afraid for him to go through this winter without them, on account of his leg." Ma sighed as she spoke.

"Yes, we'll have to spare money for that," Pa agreed. "And Susan should have shoes since she's goin' to school," he added.

"Can't I have some shoes too?" Hank wanted to know.

Pa took hold of the child's hand—not answering his inquiry.

But Hank's mother said, "If there's money enough."

The little fellow was satisfied, but Mrs. Malcolm was afraid there would not be enough money for shoes for Hank—not this winter.

16

After Winter—Spring

That winter seemed longer and harder than usual, though spring came a little early actually, yet none too soon to please the Malcolm family. Ma had been confined much of the time to the little log house with the two younger children for two reasons: Toby still had the sickness, and Hank had no shoes to cover his bare feet and keep them from the winter's cold.

The sale of the cotton had paid the actual bills, including the last note to Henry. And, although only Susan got shoes, with no more notes to pay on the farm things seemed better; and hopes for a more promising future could be seen.

Back during the winter Pa petted and talked to his fine heifers, a few of which already had calved early that spring. Wood had to be cut for the big open fireplace so that Ma and the little ones could keep warm. While working in the woods Pa talked with the little woods creatures as he walked among the pretty trees that would be timber for the sawmill before long, bringing in some more cash to help meet their needs. Yes, now that spring had arrived, things looked brighter ahead.

Occasionally, through the cold months, Ma had been able to slip away from the house and enjoy the

17

wonderful out-of-doors with Pa. There were even occasions when the children could be out on warmer days such as always spot the winter months.

Although Toby got well before the winter was over, the paralyzed leg was shorter than the other, and much smaller, and he had a decided limp. But Tom and Valinda often spoke of their thanks for his recovery and made no complaint about the very noticeable impairment. Lovable little Hank was happy that he could be outdoors, now that Toby was well.

Spring brought planting time. Pa plowed and disked the garden for Ma until the dirt was almost pulverized. The newly plowed soil smelled good. In a pit at the edge of the garden Ma kept her potted plants through the winter. There she kept also the planted seed pans for early garden plants. She squatted near a pan of cabbage plants, selecting some larger ones for the rows that were being prepared. Hank squatted beside her and started pulling at the plants. Valinda pushed his hands away. She laughed at his persistence. Toby tried to follow Pa and called out to the mule, "Gee!" when actually Pa might want the mule to go the other way. However, the animal knew Pa's voice and his tug on the reins and obeyed him rather than the little one who stumbled and fell many times in the plowed rows, crying when it hurt, but brushing dirt from his jeans and following again.

Valinda smiled as she pulled the plants from the seed pans. She thought of how the garden would keep them supplied with food—good, nourishing food. During the summer months many of the vegetables from the garden as well as berries picked from the fencerows and from the woods would be canned and kept for the winter's supply. They ate well, Valinda knew, because of thrifty management. The preparations were fun as well as being a chore.

Come June and July, the family would gather berries to dry and store. Even the little ones looked forward to all this—especially berry picking, in spite of the thorns pricking fingers, and the chiggers that buried themselves under the skin and caused itching and irritation. Ma knew just how to care for all such ailments and ills.

And for Tom and Valinda, berry-picking time was a change from the field work. They loved every minute out under the limbs of the stately trees. It was pure delight to open the lunch basket at noon and spread a picnic feast for the family. Crumbs were thrown by the young ones to tempt the birds that sat fussing at them from nearby bushes. The squirrels were so used to Pa's presence in the woods that they were nearly tame, and often one would come almost near enough to be fed by hand. That always delighted the noisy, squealing children.

Valinda brushed the dirt from her skirt and got up. She carried the basket of seedling plants to the garden. Hank, clamoring to help, followed.

Pa had three designated rows ready. Walking beside the first row, Ma dropped the plants on the ground—just the right distance apart. When all the seedlings were dropped for the three rows, she went back to make little holes in the rows in which to set the tiny rootlets. Having planted the rootlets she pressed the moist soil firmly around each seedling.

At last the three rows had been planted. Ma straightened up, placing her hands on her hips with her thumbs pressing into her tightened back muscles.

As she surveyed the rows, she uttered a cry of dismay. Every plant she had so carefully planted lay on top of the ground beside the place where she had so painstakingly put it. Ma realized that as fast as she had set out the seedlings, her little helper, following close at her heels, had pulled each one up.

The first time Hank's mother had set the plants, it had been a pleasure. Now it would be WORK to reset them, but it would have to be done. However, first she had another job to do now—a very important duty. Picking up the little fellow and turning him in the proper position across her knee, Valinda Malcolm applied a heavy hand to the seat of Hank's pants, stinging the palm of her own hand.

Hank wailed loudly. When he could hush long enough to speak, he cried out, "Why didn't you put 'em where I couldn't reach 'em?"

One afternoon Ma sat on the porch near the kitchen doorway. A starched, well-ironed apron covered her blue calico dress. In spite of the lines in her young face, and her hands made rough by having them in much water and soap, there was something about her that was worth notice. Her mother was Indian. That accounted for Valinda's high cheekbones and the dark, straight hair that she arranged becomingly, parting it in the middle and making a neat ball low on her neck. Working outside in the field gave her a glow of health. But, actually, her skin was tanned only enough for good color.

Ma was pretty. Or, she could be if she could only dress up a little better. Pa had told her he was going to dress her up fine when he could sell enough calves and cotton—enough more, that is, than was needed for other things. Perhaps Ma was dreaming of that as she sat there working the stick of the old-fashioned crock churn up and down to make the butter come.

Just then little Hank passed the doorstep and woke her from that reverie. She looked up to smile at him, her very likeness. The child continued to play close by, and Valinda Malcolm went back to some more churning and dreaming.

"Why did we name the child after Tom's brother?" she wondered. "It would have been much better to have called him Martin—looks more like my brother than Tom's, anyway," she reasoned. "My brother would have felt it an honor to have the young un named after him." Her musings drifted to the man who bore Hank's name before Hank did. "Henry doesn't care the snap of his finger about havin' the little un named after 'im. Why he—" Then Ma remembered again. "Forgive me, Lord, and forgive Henry," she prayed.

"Look at me feedin' my birds," Hank called to his mother. The child had heard his father speak of the chickens as "birds," and he was imitating. "See me?" Hank called again. "I've been out to the barn, and Pa gimme a pocketful of corn."

Ma spoke some words of notice to the boy. The chicks had lost their mother because the hen had gone off to lay. They were left to make their own living. Because the chicks found it easier to get a meal this way, they preferred to eat the corn that Hank dropped in front of them than to scratch for worms in the orchard or to search for bugs.

Ma gave a grunt as she picked up the heavy churn and started inside. The butter had come, and she would take it out into a mixing bowl to wash and mold. The buttermilk would be poured into an earthen jug to be set down at the spring to keep cool and sweet.

Just as she poured the buttermilk and set the churn onto the table, a scream from Hank got her attention again. She hurried to the door to see what had happened. By the time she was near enough to see, her brother, about whom she had only minutes before been thinking, arrived on the scene and hovered over the loudly bawling child, making an effort to assure him that he wasn't *half* killed. Arriving unannounced but just in time, he told Valinda he had seen one of the chickens become bold enough to eat from Hank's hand, and the chick had pecked sufficiently hard to cause pain but not enough to bring very much blood. Hank had been frightened and angry.

When Martin Tower told his sister what had happened, Valinda laughed heartily with him. But little Hank did not see the funny side. He went away with his pride hurting more than his hand.

"I guess that's one time my baby was glad to see you," Mrs. Malcolm said. Her statement called to remembrance the time when Martin had played Santa Claus and his costume had frightened Hank. For that reason Hank did not usually have much use for his uncle Martin. But this time he did.

"Where's the Old Man?" Martin asked, referring to Tom.

"They're at the barn," his sister answered.

"Did you say 'they'?" Martin asked her. Then, "Oh yes," he went on. "That Toby likes to keep about with Tom—and he gets about mighty well on that crippled leg." Martin went to the barn, while Valinda finished her task with the butter in the churn.

With a little cedar paddle she scooped up the butter. "Reckon Martin wants Tom to practice shootin' with the guns today. Good for 'em—crops is laid by and the berries is in the jars, and Pa orter take time off. Both of 'em's good gunsmen." Ma had surmised correctly, for Martin had come for a little practice shooting with Tom. He had his gun with him when he came upon Hank in his trouble with the chicken, and he had laid the gun on the bottom step.

Valinda had just shaped the butter into a small block and gave it a whack with the cedar paddle when she heard a loud noise outside. It was, she knew, the bang of a gun. She listened, more or less stunned. She stepped to the door to make sure. And there on the ground, leaving no doubt, lay the thing that had made the noise. Smoke rose from the end of the barrel. What more evidence did she need? But no one was around now.

"Who shot that gun?" Ma said aloud, and with anxiety in her tone, she repeated, "WHO SHOT THAT GUN?"

Mrs. Malcolm nervously and quickly edged a little farther out onto the porch, her fears mounting. There was a hole in the ground that must have resulted from the explosion of the gun. But WHO did it? Where was Hank? Ma was definitely alarmed. Then she heard a voice that caused her to look toward the barn. There, in the doorway, stood Tom and Martin with Toby wedged between them.

"Who shot that gun?" came the demanding voice of Tom.

Seeing that Tom did not know the cause of the gunshot, Valinda became more frightened, and she dropped to a chair. She could not answer her husband. The two men leaped from the barn door, and Toby came tagging behind, crying and limping as he ran.

When Tom and Martin reached Ma, her only words were, "Where's Hank? Oh, where's my baby?"

Could Hank actually have shot the gun? Could he have done that? Without further word the two men began to look for the suspect.

"I had such a time with Toby last winter," Ma sobbed, "and now Hank—oh, where is he?"

Pa did not have time to stop to console Ma, for, seemingly, his business was first to find the child. But as he moved past his frightened companion, Ma did hear him say, "It's the ground that's been shot, not Hank. Effen he had hold of the trigger he couldn't uv been in front of the barrel." His words became less audible to her ears as he went on, but she did make out that he was saying, "Effen he'd a got shot, he likely couldn't uv got out of our sight."

Ma, feeling somewhat relieved at Pa's words, began to search for Hank too. "Crawl under the house," she commanded Toby, who had grabbed her skirt when she stepped off the porch. But Toby was too frightened to do anything. Although he did not yet sense what all the excitement was about, his actions showed he knew something was wrong.

Tom ran to look in the smokehouse.

Jerking herself loose from Toby, Valinda dropped to her knees and started under the house. Her brother Martin prevented her. He crawled a short way under himself and then stopped, no doubt to let his eyes get accustomed to the darkness. Presently Martin's eyesight became keener, and through the darkness, he saw a bit of movement. Focusing his eyes on the object, he saw a little fellow backed up in the recess of the chimney footing, his knees doubled up under his chin, and two chubby, short arms clutching his legs lightly to his body.

"You rascal!" Martin scolded. "Come here." Then, calling to the others, he said, "Here he is. And he's all right."

Then calling to Hank he commanded, "Come out from there." Martin was a bit impatient and continued, "He won't budge, and I don't see no use of me goin' under."

When Pa gave certain threats, the youngster came with rapid pace, crawling on all fours.

"Don't spank me. Please, don't spank me!" He begged.

To Ma it seemed like minutes before her baby reached her. As soon as he was close enough, she extended one hand and pulled him out. Then, sitting up on the step, she lifted the child onto her lap and hugged him until it hurt. Then Ma began to cry, letting her tears drop all over the rescued youngster, who did not appear to like it a bit. He wiggled off Ma's lap and ran around the house out of sight.

"It's all my fault. I left that gun there," Martin said.

"You needn't feel that way about it," Pa said. "You ain't to blame for the accident."

"If I'm not to blame, who is? When a feller's foolin' with a gun, he should keep a level head," Martin said. "I left the gun there when I went to the barn. Laid it down when I helped Hank with his hurt hand, and left it lying there on the doorstep. Bad business when a little chap's around."

In the meantime, Toby had scooted off in the direction his younger brother had gone.

That First Automobile Ride

The automobile had existed for several years, though as far as the residents of Oak Valley were concerned, it was a thing heard of and much discussed, yet actually seen by only a very few.

Then one summer Dr. Hosea bought an automobile—a black, shining new Maxwell. He told Tom Malcolm about it when they happened to meet one day. The doctor planned to use his new car on roads that would be as passable as the one by the Malcolm home, he told Tom, adding that over some roads he would still have to use the buggy drawn by his fine horses.

On their farm in Oak Valley, Hank and Toby, six- and seven-year-olds now, were having fun playing on the bank near the road one day. There having been a recent rain, the soil was just right for frog house making. The boys busied themselves patting the mud—piling it just right around their bare feet—and had not noticed an approaching "sput, sput, sput" noise. Had they not been so involved in their frog house building, they would have noticed; for such a noise was entirely unfamiliar to their community.

But now the sputtering loomed up almost upon them. It zoomed past. It was gone before they could get a good look. Without a word between them, both boys jumped, tearing up the mud houses around their feet. They gave a spring that landed them across the ditch by the road. Both boys fell onto their hands and feet but quickly righted themselves and broke into a run, side by side. The thing was out of sight before they could get into the road. But, if possible, they would catch it and take a good look. Their imaginations were far greater than the possibilities.

Dashing ahead of Toby, Hank took the lead. Toby could not keep up, since his one leg was shorter than the other. Hank meant to track the thing by the odor left behind. Now and then Hank stooped as if smelling the scent from the track the tires had made on the sandy road. The boy would give a yelp like a dog. Toby would nearly catch up to Hank while he stopped to take another smell.

Finally, the little fellows became wise to the fact that they could never gain enough speed to catch up with what was Dr. Hosea's car, and the youngsters turned round to retrace their tracks home.

Valinda Malcolm had heard the noise of the car in time to come out to the front porch and see it as it passed. She had also seen the chasers as they left the bank to run after the automobile. She laughed at them when they appeared in the yard to tell her the news.

Ma stopped them with "Wash yer hands and set here on the steps and bide yer Pa's comin' to dinner." Not entirely ignoring the desire she knew the boys had to tell her what they had seen, she added, "Let me finish settin' the food on, and then I can listen to you." Walking back into the kitchen, she muttered, "Horseless carriage! Horseless carriage! It's beyond me too. No wonder them young uns ran to catch up with it. I'd like to set my eyes on it real good."

Valinda finished the preparations for the meal quickly. "I'll have this settin' on the table in no time." She spoke aloud to herself. "When I've finished, I'll set out on the porch with 'em and watch. Maybe that thing'll come back by." Valinda felt as excited as the two boys. "I'm gettin' lazy these days with no field work to do. Come fall, I won't have much time for idling around. Right now I'd like to see that horseless carriage come by again."

Just as she had promised the boys, and herself as well, Ma went to the porch to sit down. She dropped herself onto a cushion that covered the rawhide seat of a rocking chair. But Valinda found herself getting up about as quickly as she had sat down, for the same noise she had heard a little while ago came sounding from around the thicket up the road a little way. "Yonder comes Dr. Hosea's horseless carriage again." But the boys did not hear all she said, for they had bounded off toward the road.

Dr. Hosea turned into the lane that led right up to the yard gate. Valinda stammered and stuttered in surprise. Dr. Hosea grinned at her.

"It's nothing to be ashamed of," Dr. Hosea said at Ma's embarrassment as he leaned farther over the door of the car. "Of course you want to see my new automobile, and I feel glad. That's why I came by. I wanted to show it to you." The doctor smiled showing his own thrill about his automobile. "Come on out," he invited, "and take a real close look."

Ma obeyed, and when she reached the owner of the automobile, the children were already there. "I've been up the road to see Aunt Molly again," the doctor told her. He always explained when he stopped, for the Malcolms seemed to want to know about his visits. "I wanted to come back by and see if these little gentlemen here would like to have a ride with me." The doctor nodded at his little patient whom he still had reason to believe he had cured, for Ma never told him her secret. Then he patted Hank on the head. "You just won't ever get sick enough to have me give you any medicine," he told the little fellow.

"Aunty Molly just won't leave that fat meat alone. I tell her about it every time I go to see her," the doctor said, speaking again about the patient he had just seen. "She just says, 'I shore do love that stuff.'" The doctor smiled, then stepped out of the automobile to join the group as they admired his Maxwell. "How do you like it?" he questioned.

Ma did now know what to say. Really the automobile didn't look too much different from the buggy belonging to the Malcolm family, except that it was newer and it did not have shafts for hitching a horse to. Ma did stroke the shiny black fenders nearest her.

Toby slipped around to the back. Maybe he could discover where the smell came from—the smell Hank had been trying to track. He got real close to the back tires and sniffed.

"Where's Tom?" the doctor asked. Ma was about to tell him that Tom was due back from the field at any time, when they saw him coming, waving his hat in greeting. His smile stretched from ear to ear.

After Pa joined them, it was not hard to persuade Ma to get in the car for a ride. She was afraid, but she didn't mind as much with Pa near her. She hoped nothing would happen to them. Hesitantly, but surely, she climbed to the backseat, with Tom getting in beside her. Toby and Hank scrambled up onto the front seat beside the driver.

The motor coughed and vibrated as the doctor pushed down the accelerator and let out the clutch so that the car would start moving. He had kept the motor idling while they talked and did not have to use the hand crank for starting the motor again. Round the grove they went, the car picking up speed until it was making twenty-five miles an hour.

"Not so fast," begged Ma, leaning foward as if ready to jump.

Toby and Hank giggled. Hank was too shy to say very much, but Toby would have been talking with every breath, except that the jolts made it hard for any of them to talk.

The ride was much too short to please the appreciative boys, that was plain. Plainly, too, Ma was glad to be back home and out on the ground again. "That was too fast ridin' fer me." She smiled, but meant that for her expression of gratitude, nevertheless.

Now the Malcolms had both seen the new automobile and had had their first ride. All the Malcolms, that is, except Susan. Susan had missed the ride. Every chance little Miss Malcolm had, she went over to Piney to visit with Grandma Tower. She loved listening to Granny's tales of Indian life, and to the stories about the days of slavery. A very unhappy little girl listened when she returned home and the boys told her of their thrilling experience.

Crossing Old Sandy

It was June. Before the sun rose, Ma and Pa Malcolm had started off to town. They had left Susan in charge at home. Susan had busied herself ever since Ma and Pa had gone, with the things Ma had instructed her to do. Now she hung the shuck mop on the rack at the smokehouse. She propped her hands on her hips and stood gazing at nothing in particular. The sun rose slowly, creeping inch by inch until it was well above the willows that shaded the spring at the foot of the trail. A mockingbird sat on the gatepost of the garden fence. It broke into song with such a shrill note that Susan turned quickly to look at it. The winged visitor then sang in sweetest notes and flew away into the nearby thicket.

Having been influenced by the singing of the mockingbird, Susan lifted her own voice softly with the words, "In the sweet by and by, we shall meet on that beautiful shore." Then she paused. "I wonder if Pa and Ma are just about to get to the river." She spoke aloud. "I'm like Granny." She laughed. "I guess I should not talk to myself, but it helps when one is alone. I wish I could have gone with Pa and Ma."

Susan turned quickly on her heel and rushed into

31

the house again. "I'll wake Toby and Hank," she declared. "They'll be company." Opening the door to the boys' room, Susan looked in at the two sleepy-eyed youngsters sitting up in bed—tall little Toby and chubby Hank, not like brothers at all.

"Guess I'll not have to wake you after all," she said to them. "It's time to get up, though. Ma told me to let you sleep late since they would not be here. I've finished all the chores that they left for me to do."

"Where've they gone?" Toby wanted to know, and his lips began to curl for a cry.

"Why didn't they wake us? Why, why—?" But Hank didn't seem to know why what.

"You couldn't have gone with them," Susan answered. "And besides, they didn't know they were going until they woke early this morning. They called me before it was day, and I helped 'em get away." The boys sat silently, as if disappointment weighed down upon them—both of them.

"Get up now," Susan commanded. "And when you do, you can make your bed, if you both work at it together. I was making mine alone when I was only seven years old, and you are nine and eight."

"But you're a girl," retorted Toby.

"And you never did tell us where Pa and Ma went," Hank said.

"To town," Susan told them.

"To Benston?" Hank asked, and his eyes lighted up. In spite of his disappointment he began reasoning with a big smile spreading over his face, "To buy somethin'—somethin' for us! Some new clothes, maybe!" Then both boys squealed with excitement and jumped from bed, as if they had guessed for sure.

"Get dressed, now," Susan ordered and left the

boys' room. "Your breakfast will be ready by the time you are ready for it." As Susan closed the door, they heard her say, "No doubt Pa and Ma are just riding up to the banks of the river."

Susan could not have made a better guess, for just about that time Tom and Valinda drove Kate up to the big oak that stood with roots reaching out over the bank and feeling out into the waters of Old Sandy. Pa tightened up on the lines. Kate chewed at the bit in her mouth and came to a standstill.

Tom climbed out of the carriage and then cautioned Valinda, "Careful now," as she climbed down. Tom held her hand, lightening her step to the ground. He smiled with pride at his young wife, who actually showed fewer years in her face now than she had years before, when they still owed Henry money and when Toby had polio.

Valinda, though stiff from the long ride, walked to the horse's head to be near her husband while he tied Kate to the tree and placed plenty of sweet hay in front of her. Then taking a big carrot from the bag on her arm, Valinda lovingly handed it to Kate. "There's another in the cellar waiting for you when you take us back home," she promised.

It was only a few steps to the bank of Old Sandy. Before Pa untied the rope that held the crude boat they would use for crossing the river, he helped his wife get seated on the plank that served as a seat in the front part of the boat. He made sure there were two oars, then stepped in, rocking the boat with his unsteady step. A fish splashed the water and swam away, losing itself to their sight under the wave the boat had made. Overhead, birds that had been frightened by the appearance of people fluttered their

3—P.F.

wings and flew away to find new perches.

"Now, Pa, don't *you* fall into the river," Ma said, moving a bit to help balance the boat. Pa sat down on the rough plank seat in the middle of the boat and took the oars. Soon he had the boat moving toward the other side of the river.

The breeze blew softly, and hardly a leaf stirred. With no wind, rowing was easy. The quiet ripple of the water, the splash of the oars, and a few bird calls among the trees they were leaving behind them were the only noises. The blue of the sky, the green and slight variation of coloring of the leaves of the trees that lined the banks of the river and reflected in the water made a most restful scene.

"Ain't God good, Pa," Ma spoke reverently. "He gives us the beauty of nature, and so many good things. Pity we don't take the children to church more'n we do, and teach them more from the Good Book. They need to know more about God. I know they do. We've been powerful busy and ain't took time for spiritual things."

"They's a lot we need to learn our own selves," Pa nodded.

"Well, you do read the Bible mighty reg'lar, but that ain't enough. We oughtta go to church too. Only we'd have to go clean over to Larsen to a church."

The sun was high in the sky when the Malcolms stepped out of the boat onto the far bank of Old Sandy. It had been a peaceful and not-too-warm ride across the water. The short walk into Benston would not be bad. A great deal of shade would offer its comfort as they walked along the path into town.

Not until they started up into the main road did Ma notice that Pa had not shaved his beard before they left home. Suddenly she stopped in her tracks and scolded sharply, "Tom Malcolm, do you want me to go into town with you, and you lookin' like this?" In spite of the playful reprimand about his plight, she smiled a little, then held up a looking glass.

"Oh, you don't need to show me," Tom told his wife. "I know I didn't shave. I had a purpose. I've decided I'm a-gonna make this a *special* trip today. We ain't had much luxury in all our lives, and now I'm gonna have a barbershop shave. Yes, ma'am, I am—*today.*"

Ma chuckled heartily, then nodded her approval. "You deserve it, Pa. You shore do."

The time it took to walk the half mile from the river to the streets of Benston did not seem very long—not to Ma, even though she slowed Pa in his pace somewhat. In Benston there were not many streets, but the town was nearly double the size of Larsen. It was a bit unfamiliar to the Malcolms, for they had not often had opportunity of getting that far from home.

"I'll find a barbershop right straight and get a shave while you do your buying in the stores," Tom suggested to his wife. "When I meet you, you'll be proud of your man, you will." Pa patted a loving good-bye touch on Ma's arm.

Ma did not smile at her husband's suggestion, for she felt a bit of strangeness as she realized she would go alone into the stores that were larger than the ones she was accustomed to. She would not know the clerks as she did those in Larsen. On the other hand, she was a bit pleased that she could shop alone, for she knew what she wanted to buy and would just a wee bit rather make her own selections. So, she went her way and did not protest Tom's going his.

It was a full hour and a half before Tom and Valinda met again in front of the town hall. "Valindy," Pa spoke almost in a whisper as soon as he was near enough to be heard by the woman coming to meet him. He looked this way and that. "I've jest heerd somethin' that'll shock the wits outta you. It's about Henry."

Valinda saw that Pa did not show signs of trouble; and since she had bought some cheese and crackers and a few other little tidbits they liked to eat, she thought the news could wait until they were seated on one of the benches at the side of the building. And, anyway, nothing about Henry could shock her, she thought.

When they were settled for the noon snack, Ma offered Pa some of the food and said, "Now tell me about what you heerd—and I hope it's good." But Valinda Malcolm doubted any news that concerned Henry would be good.

Pa chuckled. "Not bad news. And, maybe," he drawled, "it ain't nothin' to get all 'roused up about, neither."

They both took bites of the food and swallowed. Ma had bought bottles of pop for them to have with the food; and when Pa had gulped down a good portion of the fruit-flavored liquid, he took another mouthful of food and began to talk between the chews. "In the barbershop, I heerd some folks a-talkin' about Henry, and—"

"Did you tell 'em you wuz his brother?" Ma asked, interrupting.

Pa swallowed again, and it was easier for him to talk. "Jest you wait, woman," he ordered. "No. Thinks I to myself, I'll learn more by listenin' than a-talkin'. Besides, if I told 'em, they might not say so much. So,

I jest kept quiet and let them talk back and forth, and I listened with both ears open to catch every word."

Valinda's curiosity was growing a little now. "Go on," she urged when Pa stopped to take a big bite of his sandwich.

"They wuz talkin' about Henry bein' so rich, and wonderin' who he'd leave what he has to, seein's he ain't got no young uns. Then one of 'em up and said he'd heerd that Henry planned to deed some land, or make a will, or somethin' to Hank, since Hank was his namesake—and maybe to Toby as well."

"And you still did not tell 'em who you was?"

"I didn't tell 'em nothin'."

"Tut, tut," Ma said. "Henry Malcolm's not gonna do nothin' like that." But she did secretly wish that something good would come of what Pa had told her. She did not want what belonged to Henry for herself and Tom, nor for her children, either. But, maybe after all, Henry was obligated to them. At least he'd taken Tom's portion of their father's property.

Of course, they did not put a great deal of faith in barbershop news, but this certainly brought something for Pa and Ma to think about. And maybe it was something they could actually hope for.

As they talked on, there was an unexpected rumble overhead, and a slight darkening of the sky. Tom looked up. "Looks like a cloud's gatherin'," he said.

Valinda became slightly uneasy, and they made ready to start for home. The bundles of purchases Ma had made were not heavy enough to be burdensome. And, with Pa assisting her in carrying her packages, they hastily covered the little way back to the river.

Soon after they were in the boat, the wind began to rise, whipping up waves which made the going rough and dangerous. The whitecaps looked frightening to Ma; and while she did not usually become upset easily, she was human, and she now showed nervousness. Very few words were spoken between the two of them, but many things could easily fill the minds of the parents as Pa stroked hard at the oars, rowing the boat across. How would anyone know what became of them if they should drown? Were they ready to die? Did they want to die? What would become of the children if they were left alone? They knew something about prayer, and Ma said a few audible words in petition to the One above them who only could protect.

After twice the necessary time usually taken to cross Old Sandy, the two thankful people stepped out of the rocking boat onto land that looked mighty good to them.

"Here we are, Kate," Ma spoke to the waiting horse, her voice rather shaky and quivering.

Kate neighed her greeting, and Pa declared the horse smiled, for she raised her head and shook it affectionately as soon as they got near her.

Seated in the carriage once more and riding toward home, Pa observed, "The clouds ain't too close on us, and I believe we'll make it in ahead of the rain."

"The wind's mighty high, and the clouds're thickenin' powerful fast," Ma answered. "But I'm glad we're acrost the river now."

Kate trotted briskly, and the trip home, after they had left the river, was made in shorter time than it had been made early in the morning from home to the river. The winds calmed a bit after a while, and the clouds lay back of them. Fifteen minutes short of the time they had allotted themselves, the buggy turned the bend around the thicket, and Pa and Ma saw three waiting children jump from the edge of the front porch. The children ran to meet their parents.

"It seems like you've been gone a whole week, instead of just a day." Susan greeted them.

Pa put the horse in the stable. He hung the harness in the shed and pulled in the carriage. Ma dragged her weary self into the house, with the three anxious youngsters pulling at her skirt. They grabbed at the packages, anxious to see what was inside the wrappers.

But, though the five of them were half starved, no tales of the day were told, nor even supper eaten, until each child had tried on the new clothes and had played a little with the special toy brought for each.

Supper over, the Malcolm family quieted down and soon the youngsters went to bed. "I bet them young uns won't go to sleep, thinkin' about their new things." Pa chuckled a little, but Ma didn't hear, for the rain was beating down upon the housetop. Besides, she was plumb tired out and was almost asleep herself. She and Pa decided to turn in too.

Some time later, Valinda Malcolm said to her husband as if she were thinking out loud, "Do you remember the day we went to Benston and you went to the barbershop over there, and the storm threatened us as we crossed the Sandy on our way home?" Ma didn't wait for an answer, talking almost without catching a breath. "And you heerd that talk about Henry's idea for giving some land to Toby and Hank? Remember?"

Tom did another whittle on the ax handle he was making before he spoke. "Of course," the man assured her. "It ain't been but a few weeks ago." Pa did not tell Ma that he had been thinking about the same thing.

"But—well," Valinda started again, wishing Tom would talk a little more about it even if it might always just be a daydream idea. "Do you reckon Henry's done anything about it—about a deed or anything?" The mother felt that it was only right that Henry should do something for their children, seeing that he never did anything to repay them for what he had done when the elder Malcolm died.

"A pretty head like yours shouldn't bother about a thing like that. Wait till you hear it has happened" was the answer Pa gave.

And that was that.

At the Ol' Swimmin' Hole

Summer had come, indeed! Could two boys think of anything better than going to the swimming hole? The parents heard Toby saying to his brother, "Hey! Let's go swimmin'!"

Pa winked at Ma, and they both chuckled. The boys were around the house near the orchard. Hank jumped from his perch on the top rail of the fence and started on a run. "I'll ask Ma," he called back over his shoulder.

Hank ran back to report to Toby, but he heard Pa caution, "Stay close to Toby. You're not very good at swimmin'."

Ma, remembering that Hank was still afraid of water, set her mending basket down and, hurrying through the house, went to the side window to watch. She pulled back the ruffled curtain and leaned out to call, "Toby, please look after Hank. He ain't learned to swim, you know." Ma feared for Hank's safety but depended heavily on Toby at times like this. She watched the two boys dash down the road. Toby was always a little behind his brother because of his one leg that was much shorter than the other. At last they were out of sight.

"Going to the Thorne house to get Peter, no doubt." Valinda laughed as she thought of the three swimming together.

The Malcolm boys did go to the Thorne house to get Peter to go swimming with them. Then the three boys cut across the field in the direction of the pasture, and on to the swimming hole. The sun beamed down on them, but they braved that. Soon they would be splashing in the cool water. The stones that had lain in the sun for hours burned their bare feet, but that didn't stop them. They did hurry to reach the shade, however, and then walking was much easier.

Perspiration ran in streamlets over their bodies. The children had been told of the danger of going into the water when that hot; so they sat under the white oak to cool off for a few minutes, fanning themselves with their ragged straw hats.

Toby pulled off his shirt first. Then off came Peter's. Two pairs of jeans were slung over a bush nearby. Toby and Peter hit the water about the same time; then they moved out into the deeper part. Hank, not quite as daring, sat dabbling his feet in a stream running from the swimming hole. He had not stripped himself as quickly as Peter and Toby, though after a time he did edge slowly into the water.

"Come on in," Peter called. "Don't be a sissy."

"I'm only being careful," Hank argued, not seeming at all pleased at being dubbed a "sissy."

Toby showed apprehension about Peter. That boy could get evil ideas in his head, and it was best to stop him before he got something started. "Hey, Peter," Toby called to the boy. "I'll race you to the old stump yonder."

"We can't do that, and you know it," was the answer; and Peter stayed suspiciously near Hank, showing no interest in the race, though they had swum that far time and again.

"Come on. Let's try, anyway," urged Toby.

Both the boys made a start, but Peter lagged a little behind, not seeming to try very hard. Hank followed them, wading slowly and getting into water up to his armpits. Venturing no farther, he turned to go back to the bank. Just as he had his back turned, something grabbed at his waistband. Hank yanked in an effort to pull away but could not release himself. Then he gave a big scream.

Toby, upon hearing his brother scream, turned and swam swiftly back. He saw Peter trying to push Hank under the water. Toby's anger began to rise.

When he reached the struggling boys, Peter had just dunked Hank. Hank came up sputtering and thrashing his arms. Toby gave Peter a stunning slap on the back, and the bully lost his hold on the victim. Not being badly strangled from the dunking that Peter had given him, Hank began to bawl loudly, and Toby led him to the bank and sat beside him.

Peter came out of the water to join the two boys sitting on the bank. But when Peter came over to them, Toby turned on him again. How he did it, even Toby might have a hard time explaining. However, the crippled boy fell with the full force of his small body and knocked the prankster to the ground. Toby put up a fight—a real fight—and won. He said not a word. What he did was enough. Peter seemed to get the message.

The three sat for several minutes then, making no move to go home or back into the water. However, as it is with boys, it all soon blew over; and the whole thing seemed to be forgotten for the time. The boys found themselves back in the water, acting as if nothing had happened. Peter swam away, but Toby stayed near Hank and did a bit of teaching him the art of swimming. Hank became less shy, and began to swim a little.

Now the boys noticed that the sun had dropped well below the taller trees, making welcome shade across the path. Without a word they dressed, and then with leaps and bounds and yelps, the three started homeward.

No mention was made of the afternoon's incident. Some things, the three boys knew, were best not talked about.

Hank, now ten years old, was certainly old enough to go fishing at the creek alone. He knew where to go for worms that could be used for bait. He and Pa and Toby had dug there many times when they had gone fishing together. The boy marched himself right off to the garden with a hoe on his shoulder and a tin can in his hand. However, his sister, Susan, met him and offered her assistance as he went through the gate.

"Oo-ooo!" the girl shrieked when she picked up the first squirmy, slimy thing. She pranced about and dropped the worm on the ground. "I can never pick up these nasty, wiggly things!" she said, but her brother's look of disgust must have made her change her mind. She made another attempt to hold the next one long enough to give it a pitch toward the container, careful with her cast. She aimed well. But when she tried with the next one, she failed. Another try met with less success, and she gave up. "Let *me* dig and *you* pick them up," she suggested.

"Aw, you can't dig," Hank protested, "You've been so prissy of late. I've noticed it. I think it's because you was promoted to go to Larsen to school next year. You're plain sissy."

"You don't appreciate what I'm doing to help you. You just wish you were ready to go to Larsen yourself," Susan accused. "You're jealous."

"Not me. I'm not jealous. I'm quittin' school, and for good, when I finish at the little brown schoolhouse." Then Hank made some more accusations about Susan's air of sophistication.

His sister showed anger and stepped back, stumbling against a big flint rock. She sat down abruptly and winced in pain. Tears welled up in her eyes.

"Good enough for you," Hank said, his words probably hurting her feelings more than the fall on the rock. He went on digging worms.

"I wish old Uncle Dave would take this rock away. I've saved it for him long enough," Susan spoke up.

"What—you saved it?" Hank laughed. "Pa saved the rock. Promised it to Uncle Dave for a doorstep when he and Aunt Doll get their house finished.

Suddenly Susan began to laugh.

"What's all that for?" Hank asked. "What are you gigglin' about anyway? I thought you wuz plenty mad about fallin'."

"I was thinkin' about Uncle Dave, how he acted when he took Aunt Doll to Benston to the hospital. Poor things. I shouldn't laugh." But Susan seemed incapable of stopping.

"How do you know how Uncle Dave acted at the hospital? You wasn't there."

"You learn a lot over the grapevine." Susan suddenly put her hand to her mouth as if to stop laughing.

"Like what?"

"Maybe I'd do as bad under the circumstances," Susan, now sobered somewhat, added with a giggle. "But it *was* funny. Aunt Doll was dreading the operation and was about to back out and come home. One of the nurses gave her something to settle her nerves. That must have made her get out of her mind, sorta, and she got to talking wildly. Uncle Dave got frightened and ran down the ramp, hobbling on that one leg of his and his peg leg, and calling to the first nurse he could see. 'Woman!' he called to her." Then Susan showed guilt in her face, and hesitating to go on, she said, "Maybe I ought not to tell this."

"You've gone this far. Might as well go on. You must be nearly through with that tale. You'll be ready to tell another when that one gets cold," Hank said sneeringly.

"Well, all right, then. Uncle Dave said, 'Woman, come here quick! Come to my woman—to Doll! She's done got so drunk that I know she's a-gonna die affore 'n ye kin git here!' "

"It wasn't really so funny after all," Hank said. And since Hank did not laugh, Susan could hardly afford to laugh again.

Remembering his mission, Hank picked up the can of bait and turned to his sister. "Please, pretty please, will you return the hoe to its place in the toolshed?" Whistling as he left her standing there, he dreamed of old Mr. Bass that he knew was in the mudhole where he would be fishing. He had seen the full length of the fish's body out of the water several times.

Nicky, the family dog, scampered along behind

46

Hank; but suddenly catching a certain scent, the little dog bounded off. Then it was Hank realized he could not now see his house. Fear pressed down upon him, and the new adventure began to lose its thrill. He almost wished Susan had come with him. She would be company, even if they quarreled sometimes. He called to Nicky, but the little dog did not come back.

The boy heard all kinds of noises. The swish of his trouser legs rubbing against each other sounded louder than usual. The birds' songs sounded scary for some reason. He heard the dry twigs as little forest creatures moved them in the close woods. It was awesome, as if something might jump from behind a bush or tree to frighten him. Yet he was determined to go on. Then the boy picked up a little trot as he started down the next valley.

Now that he had covered the distance and was sitting on a log, rigging up his cork, hook, and sinker, he almost forgot his fear. "I hope you're in there," he spoke aloud to the fish he hoped to catch. Nicky at that moment must have heard Hank speak, for he ran to him barking an encouragement.

Hank got a nibble at once, then held still to let the fish get the hook set in its mouth. Just at that instant a voice sounded behind him, making him jump; and he jerked his pole too soon. "Girls can come up at the wrongest time," the boy fussed, turning around to see Sally Boutwell approaching. "Why did you come?" he asked her. "Wasn't you afraid to come over here by yourself?"

"I saw you," the girl said, "and tried to catch up with you; but you wuz goin' too fast for me."

It did seem good to have company, and Hank tendered an invitation. "Come on and help me fish."

"Don't have anything to fish with," she told him.

"I've got plenty of bait," the little fisherman offered.

"But it'll take more'n bait," the saucy one broke in.

"Just a minute," Hank snapped. "You're gettin' pretty smart. Let me finish." Hank gouged a hole in the damp earth and secured his pole while he rigged another contraption for Sally. "I've got only one more hook," he warned her, "and you mustn't lose this one. Watch where you throw your line."

Sally took the pole fixed up for her and waited for further instruction from the boy she had followed.

"They's a good place over there," he told her. "Drop your line over by that tree limb hangin' over the water."

Sally started in the direction Hank indicated, while the boy continued to talk. "Don't try to get out on the log lying in the water, though. It's slippery, and I ain't got no time to drag a girl outta the water."

"How'll I know when I get a fish on my hook?" Sally wanted to know.

"The cork'll go under."

"Then what do I do?"

"What'll *you* do? Oh, Sally!" Hank scolded. "What else will you ask?"

"Nothing, if you don't want me to bother you." Sally pouted.

"You ain't botherin' me. Glad you come along. Call me if you get a nibble—if the cork goes to bobbin' and tryin' to go under."

Hank didn't get back to his pole before Sally yelled, calling to him loudly. He hadn't expected to be called so soon. But back to her he rushed. "Hold still," he cautioned. "I believe you've got one." The boy

48

reached for her pole. "You've got a *big* one," he said excitedly. "It's gonna be a tussle."

Pa had taught Hank about handling the pole when a fish was caught. Hank remembered. Carefully he handled the pole, pulling it gently, slowly, but firmly—giving the right amount of slack at the right time. It seemed like an hour to Sally, but in only minutes they sighted the fish as it fought under the water. "It's Mr. Bass!" Hank screamed. "You've got Mr. Bass."

Sally jumped up and down while Hank brought in the floundering thing, in spite of his motions for her to stay out of his way. Joy and disappointment showed in Hank's face. Happiness because Mr. Bass had been caught. Jealousy since he was not the one who had caught the beauty. But because his aim had been accomplished—Mr. Bass had been caught— Hank could only be grateful to Sally, and gladly he rebaited her hook. Then, with Sally going back to her stationed place, the little fisherman said longingly, "I wish I'da been the one to get 'im."

When Hank had run over to help Sally he had dropped his pole; the line and hook he now found tangled in a bush. He tried to retrieve it. The water was too deep to wade out to the brush. If he walked out on the forbidden log, he could easily get his hook untangled. But that was a risk. What should he do? Well, he had little choice. He stepped out on the log and took several steps, then his foot slipped and his body made a big splash as he fell in, splashing muddy water all about. Hank yelled.

"What's the matter?" Sally called across the distance between them. Nicky came bounding to the aid of his little master. And, when the dog had helped

49

pull the dripping boy out onto the bank, Sally noticed that his hand was bleeding.

"I'll tie up your cut for you and stop the bleeding," the girl offered as she took hold of Hank's arm, and looked at his cut hand.

"Tie it up? With what?" Hank asked. On his wet shirt sleeve he wiped the tears that came. He screwed up his face with the pain of the gash; but after all, he mustn't cry in front of Sally.

The girl jerked the rags that held her pigtail plaits. With the two rags and her skill, a neat bandage soon covered the bleeding cut, making her friend feel much better.

"I cut my hand on that jagged limb yonder," Hank explained, pointing. "Bring your fish," he ordered, "and we'll go home. It's time." He picked up the fish, and speaking more audibly than he had intended, he said, "I wish I'da caught it."

"You should have Mr. Bass; he's yours," Sally offered. Her sympathy for the fisherman showed as much as his disappointment did. And Hank could not help knowing that Sally felt nothing was too good for him.

Nicky frisked in front of the two as they went. The dog seemed to sense success had been theirs. He wagged his tail and gave little barks as if to say, "I am glad too." They hurried through the wooded area and into the clearing. Upon reaching the field they would part their ways. Sally would take a path at right angles to Hank's and enter a different road that would lead to her home.

"You take the fish," the girl suggested again as they were about to separate. But Hank hesitated, ashamed to take the only fish they had caught, and especially since he didn't catch it. However, Sally urged again, "Please keep him. He's really *yours*. Please do," she begged. "My mother doesn't like to cook fish anyway," she went on. Then she pushed the hand away that was holding the bass out to her.

Having presence of mind and good manners, Hank thanked Sally for Mr. Bass. Waving to her, he called, "Thank you for tying up my hand."

The little girl watched Hank, whom she adored, hurrying off, his eyes on the trophy in his hand, and Nicky, the dog, acting just as proud as his master. Then with a sigh she hurried off in the opposite direction.

School Days and Temptations

In the fall there was excitement in Oak Valley, especially among the children. They were to have a male teacher at the little brown schoolhouse. Now Mr. Hammer stood behind the desk that had for so many years been occupied by Miss Primm. Until then, Miss Prim had seemed to be a permanent fixture at the little brown schoolhouse.

But Mr. Hammer got off to a bad start from the beginning. He had from the first day let the pupils know that he was complete master of the place. Had that kind of situation worked elsewhere, it certainly did not work in Oak Valley. Resentment showed from one child and then from another. Mr. Hammer became somewhat confused and, seemingly, at his wit's end. He resorted to whipping some of the boys unmercifully. Toby and Hank received their share of the stripes. They, with the other boys, determined to get even with this new teacher.

Somehow little tales about the schemes that were brewing got to the parents one way and another. So, although the children were well organized, the wise parents quickly held a meeting and had the matter settled before it fell into the hands of the pupils. Mr. Hammer was relieved of his duties, and Miss Primm was asked to return to finish out the school year. Now more excitement was brewing on that October morning. Every pupil was bubbling over with gladness.

Miss Primm had gone early to the schoolhouse. She found herself looking over the list of names on the record book. Not any were new to her. There were Sally Boutwell, Mabel Stratton, and the twins—Ruth and Faith Parker. "That Hank!" she recalled as her pretty blue eyes mentally saw laughing faces rather than names on a record book. "And Toby," she said aloud, thinking fondly of him because of his handicap. Then reading on down as a smile played about her lips, she said, "He's a tough one!" She was speaking about Peter Thorne. But she was sure that Peter loved her just as did the other pupils.

The clock on the wall and a babble of small voices outside told Miss Primm that it would soon be time for school to begin. She went to the doorway to welcome the little ones and, yes, the larger ones too. Children were coming from all directions, lunch pails in their hands and books under their arms.

Hank was ahead of the rest. Chubby little fellow! His bare feet brought him fast to be the first to greet the beloved teacher. Up the steps he bounded and stuck out his broad little hand to shake his teacher's dainty one. Miss Primm felt like hugging him tight, but the child was nearly as big as she.

"Good morning." The teacher saluted all of them. "How happy I am to be with my children again!" They giggled because she had called them *her* children. Some of them came from homes where not much love existed, and they had not seemed to belong. Miss Primm showed that she wished only happiness for these children lent to her from God—lent for a season. She picked up the bell to ring it, though the group had gathered around her.

"Let me ring it" came from several voices. Miss Primm handed the bell to little Ruth Parker, one of the twins, because she was nearest to her. "Such a sweet little tot" registered on the teacher's mind. Maybe Ruth was one of her favorites. Actually, Miss Primm had twelve favorites. That's how many pupils she had.

When the bell rang, every child got into line to march in. The children did not have to be told; they just did it. Like twelve little trained soldiers the boys and girls came in and took their seats. If Mr. Hammer had slipped in, he might well have thought that there were twelve new students, as well as a new teacher, that October morning.

"We will not have to get acquainted, children," Miss Primm began. "Only Randall Walters is new in school this year, and I have known Randall since he was only *this* big." She held her hands apart to measure. "Of course, Susan and Steve are in Larsen, where some of you will be going soon."

That suggestion brought expressions from several of the pupils. It showed all over that Peter, Mabel, and Sally could hardly wait their time to go to Larsen. For the twins, it would be a long time before they could go. As for Hank, he had told Susan last summer that the little brown schoolhouse offered all the education that he would need and he still felt that way.

Because it would take a day or so to get back into the routine, not many regular lessons were held that day. Some songs were sung. Previous assignments were noted, and there was a miscellany of other things. One wanted to recite a poem; and Toby, as usual, had something funny to relate. Nearly always Hank could think of a self-made, but mostly true story. And, before the day was over, it came his turn.

Hank made his way to Miss Primm's desk. Before he could begin, giggles and laughter filled the room because he couldn't get properly situated. He propped one foot on top of the other and then reversed them. "Make 'em hush!" the boy begged and then grinned himself.

He told of a time when he had cut his finger and Ma had tied it up with a rag, saturating the rag with kerosene—her medicine. When he had been left alone, he had found some matches. And, well, matches and kerosene do not make a good mixture when the match has been ignited. Actually, the story was quite too long to be of real interest to the teacher. But Randall Walters had cried when Hank told of the burn he had experienced. Sally Boutwell's eyes told Hank that she remembered the time when she had tied up his cut hand on their fishing trip. Even Miss Primm sensed the seriousness of it when he told of the flesh that cooked on his finger before he could rub out the flame. Then Hank held up his finger to show the scar.

That afternoon, when twelve happy children went home after school, parents of Oak Valley received different children back home, for there was now a normal atmosphere at the little brown schoolhouse.

School days went on happily but uneventfully. One Sunday morning after finishing his breakfast Hank went outside and down to the railroad tracks to watch for the dinkey train. On school days he couldn't be around to see the train pass, but Sunday—this was the day!

The sun rose slowly over the trees beyond the curve. Hank was not taking particular notice of the sunrise, however. If only he could ride on the little locomotive. He had watched the puffing engine go past his place near the west side of the pasture since the sawmill workers had built the railroad that led into the woods where they were getting logs. Hank had long determined to ride into the woods on that train some day.

The train would be gone all day. Ma would miss him and worry. He knew she would. But if he let things like that stop him, he would never get that chance. If he told her, she would tell Pa, and already Pa had forbidden the boy to take a risk like that. Of course, the engineer would not agree to having a boy ride the train. But he had figured it out. The rise in the hill where he sat would slow the train to almost a turtle pace, and it would be easy for him to swing on at the back without the engineer's ever taking notice of him.

So, crouched behind a bush at the foot of the bank, Hank waited. He knew it was about time for the train to pass by. He would not have long to wait. Excitement rose in his young heart as he heard the whistle blow just yards away. Hank got onto his hands and feet, ready to make a lunge. With the passing of the engine as it reached the climb, the whole train slowed down and the cars passed slowly—more slowly as each car passed by him. One by one the flat cars went by until the last one reached the place where Hank was. Giving the right jump and grabbing hold, the boy was on the last car without any trouble.

Hank eased down onto the bed of the car and made himself as comfortable as one could be on an old jolty train. Now he was fulfilling that yearning dream, and it had been very easy. No one had seen him—or so he thought.

The sights Hank saw as he rode along were not at all unfamiliar to him. He was riding over roads he had roamed time and again, hunting and fishing, or just exploring with the other boys of the neighborhood. Nevertheless, he was riding on that train that had tempted him for these several months. Rounding the hill up which they first came, then going down, the train picked up speed, tickling the boy's stomach and causing him to giggle. Of course, the chug-chug-chugging of the train's engine sounded louder than Hank's giggles, and the engineer did not hear the boy as he laughed.

When it came to the old burned-down schoolhouse in Piney community, the train slowed, then came to a stop. Hank got nervous. He saw the engineer jump off to get chunks of wood to fire up the boiler. The community boys, as they had taken walks, had seen the piles of pine stumps and roots alongside the railway. They had known the piles were for refueling the engine. What if the engineer spied him now! He didn't want to be told to get off and go home. Oh, how he did want to go on and make the full round. "I *hope* he won't see me!" the boy breathed.

The engineer leaned over the pile of wood and picked up a chunk. Then he stopped short and dropped the piece he had in his hand. Raising his hand to shade his eyes, he spoke to the fireman, who stood beside him. Hank did not hear their words, but he did see the engineer start in his direction, leaving the fireman to load the wood. Now the big man stopped right in front of him. "What are you doing here, boy?" he bellowed out.

Hank's heart beat loudly. He was afraid the big man could hear the beating. What could he do now? "Please, sir—." He hesitated, and then told his story.

It seemed like minutes to Hank before the man said anything else. Hank moved nervously about on the uncomfortable platform. Then the engineer shook his head and turned away, then back to Hank. "I'm goin' to let you go this time, boy," he said, "but don't you let this ever happen again." The big man made a move to go back up front. "Don't tell nobody, neither. What's your name?" he asked.

"Hank," the boy muttered.

"Hank who?" the engineer wanted to know. "Kelly's my name—Chuck Kelly."

"Hank—Hank Malcolm," Hank told the engineer. With that introduction the big man left. Hank was thrilled that he would be allowed to continue the trip.

The train finally moved on. Hills, valleys, and creeks would be crossed. After the jogs and jolts for some time, the train arrived where the loggers were waiting with the mules, ready to snake up the trees that had been felled to be hauled to the sawmill in Larsen. Hank jumped off and found a place on the side of a grassy slope, where he could watch.

The work the men were doing looked hard. Nevertheless, Hank sort of wished he could be a logging man. The hours wore on. The boy got sleepy and before long his eyelids closed and he was sound asleep. He did not know how long he slept. But when he awoke, he noticed the men were unhitching the mules, the train had been loaded, and the crew was making ready to quit for the day.

The ride home was not so jolty, for the weight of the logs made riding smoother. The engine worked harder, though; and clouds of black and gray smoke belched from the smokestack. Sometimes flames came out at the top, and even tiny pieces of burning trash came out, falling by the wayside. Even though the fire died before the trash pieces fell to the ground, it looked quite dangerous to Hank. Could these things start a fire along the trail?

Hank had had a long day, fulfilling though it had been. He was glad to get back home even if he did not know what he would meet there. One thing he did know. Supper would be ready, and he was hungry. He waved his thanks to the engineer and headed for home.

In the kitchen Ma set the lighted kerosene lamp on the table. Susan helped put the food on for the evening meal. Hank tried to act as usual as he joined the family at the table, waiting for what might be said to him.

Pa made some mention of the lumber company and expressed his wish to have a job with it when he would not be busy on the farm. Hank's suspicions ran high. "Now he will say something to me for what I have done," the boy thought. Of course, he knew the family had guessed by now where he had been. However, not a word was breathed about his ride—no questions asked. The famly made casual conversation, but Hank ate his supper in silence. He thanked Ma for the good food; and still visibly jittery, got up to go to his room. Then he heard his father's voice call him.

"Yes, Pa," he said with his best manners and

waited for the reprimand.

"See that this trick never happens again." Those were Pa's only words.

Later he learned that Pa had been in the pasture doctoring a sick cow and had seen him swing himself onto the train.

A few weeks later on a midafternoon when the wind was biting cold, Hank came home from school and bounded up the steps. "I'm froze stiff," he told Ma when she met him at the door. Toby hurried along behind, not quite keeping up because of his crippled leg. Hank had not waited, for he had a plan that had been influenced by the low gray clouds.

Not many snows came to excite the children in those parts, and Hank had seen very few. However, he had learned just what clouds indicated snow. "It sure looks like snow'll come before mornin'," he shouted as he pushed past Ma. Ma held the door open for Toby.

After warming themselves by the stove for a while, Toby suggested that he and Hank should do their chores in the barn. He winked at his brother as he talked.

Passing through the kitchen, the boys grabbed biscuits from the warming closet of the cookstove. They stuck their thumbs into the still-warm bread, making holes to hold some syrup.

At the barn Hank found a hammer, nails, and some scraps of lumber—just what he needed. As for the chores, he had made a bargain with Toby to care for them. When the thing Hank had made was viewed by the two, it did not look like one that a master builder would have been proud of, but Hank was. It looked

60

pretty good to him. With it he headed for the clump of bushes in the fencerow at the near edge of the woods. That's where he had in mind to put his homemade trap.

The trapper got his rig set properly, making a canopy of thick brush and sticks in front of it, overlaying that with bits of dead grass. Grains of corn and oats were scattered, making lure for the birds the boy hoped would come into his trap. Having everything ready, he stepped back to take another look. "That'll catch a family-sized mess," he said, snapping his finger as his chest swelled with pride.

Toby was nearly through at the barn when Hank got back, and the two went to the house together. After supper the family sat visiting around the crackling fire for a while. Tom and Valinda went to bed a little early, however. "Doubt effen you young uns can go to school tomorrow," Pa called from his room. "You can sleep a little late if it suits you."

"Hurray!" came from the three who would benefit from Pa's suggestion.

"Think snow will be fallin' shortly," their father added. "Not fit weather for you to be out, dressed no more'n you are for such weather."

Soon deep snoring announced that the Malcolm parents were asleep. Susan sat up until the logs burned in two and fell in the middle between the andirons. The red coals darkened and went into ashes. The fireplace cooled faster tonight, and soon she was off to cuddle down under her bedcovers. "Goodnight," she called to the boys. She buried her head in the soft pillow.

Toby and Hank stayed up, looking a dozen times or more outside to see if the snow had yet started to fall.

However, since they did not replenish the fire, the cold soon drove them to bed too.

The snow began coming down soon after all the Malcolm family were asleep. By morning everything outside was white, and several inches of the fluffy, white, frosted rain made covering for the ground.

"Whoopee!" cried Hank when he awoke and jumped out of bed to look out the window.

"No school today!" shouted Toby, a little too loud to please Hank.

"Sh-h-h!" cautioned the other. "I want to go to my trap before Pa and Ma wake up."

Susan raised her tousled head enough to peep out, but she soon drew back under the covers. Sleep seemed more appealing to the girl than the snow. "Oooo!" She smiled to herself and snuggled deeper into the feather bed.

Hank dressed quickly and ran to the window again, this time to raise it. The cold air made him button up his jacket. Tree limbs, fences, and the ground that were bare yesterday were now glistening white. Blue jays and cardinals hopped about, adding color to the picture outside. There was the twitter of birds hunting for bugs or worms or seeds wherever food could be found. Straddling the windowsill and reaching for the tree limb that scratched his windowpane when the wind blew, Hank swung himself out and dropped to the ground, sinking ankle deep in a drift of snow. "Never've seen it this deep," the boy observed.

The sole on his shoe flapped as he lifted his foot from the snow. "Guess I better fix this thing first," he decided, and he went to the barn. He picked up a gunnysack, opened the sharp blade of his pocket knife, and ripped the sack open. Then he wrapped it around his shoe, fastening the wrapping with a nail. Since that gave such a feeling of warmth, he decided to wrap both shoes. Across the old cotton patch, past the clump of sassafras that had cooled tired cotton pickers in the early fall, the boy trudged to the edge of the woods—and to his trap.

"Ho, ho!" Hank greeted the first little creature he met. It happened to be a squirrel. "You'd better scurry back into a knothole and keep yourself warm." He threw a few grains of corn before the pretty little thing. "Want some breakfast?" he asked."Don't be scared of me. I ain't gonna hurt ya none."

Nearing the trap, he crept along a little quieter. There was a flutter of wings inside the contraption he had made the afternoon before. Joy welled up inside the trapper, and his heart beat faster with excitement. He could hardly wait to look inside. He eased himself into position so that he could look in. The sight was almost overwhelming. His trap was full of the pretty feathered things.

Tom and Valinda had not missed their younger son when they had come into the kitchen. Of course Toby kept quiet, but he did go to the door often and look out. Presently, the boy burst out with laughter that brought Pa and Ma to the door, pushing up close behind him. What a sight! Two bateaulike feet bringing a boy with a sackful of something in one hand, and some other kind of contraption in the other.

"What's he up to?" Ma asked, with eyes widening. "And what's the rig on his feet?"

"Musta got some quail last night in his trap," Toby reckoned.

"Trap? What trap?" Pa questioned. "I didn't know

he had a trap. Where did he get a trap?"

"He decided, when we came from school yesterday, he was gonna make one," Toby explained.

"And nothin' could stop him," Ma declared.

"Not with his dogged determination," Pa added, shaking his head. "And it musta paid off. But I don't go along with trappin' creatures. He'll have to turn 'em loose."

That wasn't to Hank's liking. But Pa insisted he turn the birds loose.

"Haven't ya heerd about birds bein' cared for by the heavenly Father? Not one falls to the ground without Him knowin' about it." You young uns ain't gonna trap His creatures."

And Hank knew Pa's word was law.

That Strange Family

It wasn't every day that a new family settled in the area. When one came in, all the neighbors pitched in to help it get settled. It was Susan who brought word home to Ma and Pa and Toby and Hank about the new family that had come to settle in Larsen. The name was Korrel. There were three youngsters in the family. Susan knew very little more except these people had some strange ideas. They were very religious people, she had been told.

Then one day Hank and Toby went to Larsen to sell some of the Malcolms' freshly butchered meat. This was a regular affair for Toby and Hank every time Pa butchered. The boys had accompanied their father when they were younger but now they were old enough to make the trip by themselves. They always welcomed the change from farm chores.

The boys sold cuts here and there at nearly every stop that morning. At last they came to Mrs. Todd's house.

"I don't like that woman," Toby declared. He pitched his voice high and said, "This is a nice piece of steak!" He and Hank both laughed as he pretended to be Mrs. Todd. Then he added, "Now, do you have a bone for my dog?"

65

"You sound a lot like Mrs. Todd." Hank laughed. Then he grimaced. "I wonder if there's any meat left on the bone by the time the poor dog gets it."

Toby knocked on the door, which was soon opened by Mrs. Todd. "Well, I declare, you've come with the meat," she said and followed the two boys back to the wagon, where she selected a piece of steak.

Toby looked at Hank and winked.

Hank in turn grinned broadly as Mrs. Todd asked, "Do you have a nice bone for my dog?"

When the boys found a bone for her, she took it and the steak and hurried into the house. The boys climbed on the wagon and drove off to their last place of call, the boarding house. Toby tightened the reins to stop the horse when they reached the big white house and then jumped from the wagon. He tethered the horse to the hitching post.

"Sure hope we've got enough meat for Mrs. Stagg. She's our best customer. We've sold a lot of meat this morning," Hank said as he waited for Toby to finish tying the horse's reins.

"Ya, she usually buys a half of beef. I sure like Mrs. Stagg. Say, there she is, coming out of the door."

"You boys must have got up real early this morning," Mrs. Stagg said. "Are you sleepy?"

"No, not really," Hank answered. "The fine mornin' air makes a fellow feel good. Hope we ain't too near sold out to suit you this time."

"Why, bless yer hearts," Mrs. Stagg said. "I'll just take what you have left—all of it. You won't have to deny other customers, will ya?"

"Don't you worry none," Toby told her. "Take what you want."

The boys carried the meat to the house for her.

"Say, have you had breakfast yet," Mrs. Stagg asked as she motioned where the meat should be put.

"No, ma'am. And we're half starved," Toby blurted.

Hank gave his brother a poke in the ribs, but Mrs. Stagg chuckled heartily. "Well, jest sit yourself down at the table," she ordered. She piled two plates full of food. "If you want more, there's more where this came from."

The boys ate their fill. Not a crumb was left. Hank wiped his mouth on his sleeve and got up to leave. But Toby, holding his cap against his chest, bowed his thanks for both of them. Then, running out, he jumped over the endgate of the wagon while Hank untied the horse. When they were both seated on the high front seat, Toby flipped the reins and clucked to the horse, which ambled off down the street pulling the empty wagon.

"Hey, will ya' look over there!" Hank pointed to a pigtailed girl who ran behind a tree, then stuck her head out and giggled shyly at the boys as she said, "Hi, boys!"

Toby slapped the reins' over the horse's back. "Wonder why she's callin' us. Her folks never buy meat."

"I know, she's one of them Korrels. They're funny people. They don't use meat at all. Pa says he heard they go to church on Saturday," Hank told Toby. "They call themselves Seven day Advents, or something like that. Guess that's the name of their church."

"Of what church are we?" Toby asked.

"None. But Pa and Ma read the Bible a lot. They believe in God. You know that. We're doin' all right."

The girl dodged behind another tree. This time she

smiled shyly and said, "I'd sure like to ride in your wagon."

"Girls that age is silly." Toby shrugged.

"Well, she ain't bad to look at," Hank declared. Then he laughed. "Bet her mom would whomp her good if she knowed she'd asked for a ride."

"She is sort of pretty," Toby agreed. He gave his brother a poke. "No town girl's gonna notice you though," he said slyly.

That evening as the boys went about their chores on the farm, somehow Hank kept thinking about the pigtailed girl and her impish face as she had peeked out from behind the trees. Wonder why her family is so strange. Imagine, not eating any meat and going to church on Saturday.

Hank couldn't get the thought out of his head easily about strange people who go to church on Saturday and who don't eat meat. And even in his dreams that night he saw the face of the little Korrel girl jumping out from behind trees. There was always a grin on her face, and sometimes she would say, "I'd like a ride in your wagon." Sometimes she said, "I'd like a ride to church!"

Hank went down to breakfast in the morning with a grin on his face, thinking about his dreams during the night.

No one seemed to notice him as he sat down at the table. Pa was telling Ma not to bother much about a noonday meal. There was a lot of hoeing that needed to be done that day. They would have to hurry and work hard and fast. No time to dally over a noon meal.

Ma had made a sweet-potato pie the night before. Now she suggested that the pie would be enough for the noon meal. "You all like my sweet-potato pies," she said.

The family hurried to the garden as soon as possible; and without much conversation they worked, stopping only infrequently to straighten their backs and wipe a streamlet of perspiration from their cheeks.

A few minutes before noontime Ma put down her hoe and started for the house to get the scanty lunch on the table. The others followed shortly after.

"Say, there's Brother Thrasher." Toby pointed as he and Hank began to wash up at the basin set out on the porch.

"And it looks as if Pa's invited him to stay fer lunch," Hank answered. "Pa likes to have the preacher come." He laughed. "He sure likes to be able to set Brother Thrasher right on the Bible."

"Ya know, I think Pa knows the Scriptures better'n the preacher."

The family and Brother Thrasher soon gathered around the table. Another plate was set for the preacher at the head of the table and Pa called on him to ask the blessing.

Ma set the big pan, hot from the oven, in the center of the table. Wonderful spicy odors seeped through the pierced top crust of the sweet-potato pie.

"What'll ya have, Brother Thrasher?" Pa asked, taking the man's offered plate and heaping it with a piece of the steaming pie.

Hank giggled and nudged Toby as he whispered, "What choice's the man got? Look at the butter he's piling on that pie."

Ma apologized for not having any meat, but Brother Thrasher said it didn't matter. Then he added, "We've got a family over in Larsen who don't eat meat at all."

"You mean those people that keep Saturday instead of Sunday?" Pa asked. "Don't know where they git their ideas. They sure are way off the track."

"The children all seem healthy enough even if they don't eat meat," Susan spoke up. "Guess not eating meat doesn't hurt them."

"But did ya ever hear of anyone else keepin' Saturday fer Sunday?" Hank wanted to know. "They sure are mixed up bad."

"I guess they don't read the Good Book much," Brother Thrasher added.

Pa scratched his head. "I dunno," he said. "Does the Good Book mention Saturday or Sunday? I guess we'd better think on that. Most everyone keeps Sunday; so everyone sure can't be wrong."

Pa and Brother Thrasher began to talk about other things. Soon the preacher took his leave.

Time passed rapidly. The Malcolm children were growing up. Susan finished her high school in Larsen and went away to college. The first few weeks after she left seemed as if there had been a death in the family. Ma and Pa were proud of Susan, but they missed her about the place.

Maybe because of Susan's having gone to college, Toby took to wandering. Hank guessed, however, that there was an attraction over in the Maple Hill community.

One Sunday Hank noticed Toby, all dressed up, walking stealthily away from the house. "Where ya goin'?" Hank yelled at the startled Toby.

Toby stopped in his tracks. "To see my gal—Nancy .Brooks."

To Hank's amazement he added, "Want to go with me? There's another pretty girl over there. Her name's Vera. She's my gal's friend—Nancy's friend, I mean."

Hank hadn't expected such an offer. "Ya mean I could go with you? 'Course I ain't got no interest in girls," he added quickly.

"Sure, you can come along. Vera's a town girl—just moved from Larsen to Maple Hill. Guess she wouldn't really be interested in a farm boy." Toby started to walk on, then called back over his shoulder. "She's sort of a religious girl—some strange religion!"

"Religious?" Hank repeated. "Isn't religion religion?"

But Toby had already sauntered off down the road toward Maple Hill.

Hank wandered into the house, where Ma was washing the dishes. Pa sat near the window and was reading aloud a chapter from the Good Book. Ma didn't seem to be paying much attention. She gazed out the window as she set the dishes on the oilcloth-covered table to drain. Suddenly, but dreamily, she interrupted Pa's reading.

"Looks like soon we'll be right back where we started from about twenty years ago. There'll be jes' the two of us—our young uns'll be married and gone."

Pa closed the Book and put it on the table.

Ma went on, "Don't seem no time since we wuz lookin' forward to gettin' our little uns through life—" A tear would have fallen onto the dishes had she not wiped it away with the corner of her apron.

Pa looked up startled. "I s'pose some man will be wantin' Susan's hand one of these days."

Ma sighed, "An' Toby is courtin' some girl in Maple Hill. Hank'll find some girl soon too—though he ain't actin' ready to settle down get."

"How'd you know Toby wuz goin' to Maple Hill to see a girl?" Pa wanted to know.

"I jest overheerd him and Hank a-talkin' as Toby left."

Pa sat up straight and tilted his chair back onto two legs. "Tut, tut, Valindy," her man said. "We wouldn't be alone if they marry. With each of 'em takin' a companion, that'll make six instead of three."

"You're feelin' their loss too," Ma told Pa, with an emphatic tone of voice. "Needn't try to turn it off that-a-way."

Hank, having heard a whistle from his friend Steve, hurried out of the house.

When Ma finished the dishes, the elder Malcolms walked hand in hand to the front porch. There they found Hank and Steve on the porch step. The boys had their guitars lying across their knees. "We'll sing you a song if you'd like," Hank said to his parents. Hank enjoyed his guitar, especially when he had Steve with him. The Malcolms laughed heartily at Hank's offer and agreed. The two boys started off with a song, accompanying themselves on the instruments.

The boys sang and talked. The afternoon passed rapidly. Steve reached over and plucked the strings of Hank's guitar. He rose as if to go, but sat back down. "Look!" He pointed. "Here comes Toby."

"Here comes the lone suitor," Hank teased when Toby opened the yard gate to let himself in.

"Mind your own business," Toby demanded. But when he reached the two who sat on the higher step,

72

Toby stopped before them and raised his crippled foot to rest on the bottom step. Before he started conversation with the musicians, he spoke to Ma and Pa. "Feelin' good?" he asked his parents. Then, to the guitarists, "What you playin'?" Not waiting for an answer, he went on, "A girl's over at Maple Hill with a new guitar. She wants you to teach her to play it, if you will." He was addressing his brother.

"How come you talkin' to her about guitar lessons? Is she the one you called Vera? You said she was a town girl."

"Gimme time to answer. No, she's not Vera, but her sister. I fogot her name. She and Vera are both Nancy's friends."

"How did she know I could play a guitar?"

"I told her."

"Well, the pleasure'd all be mine." Hank grinned.

Steve sat still. No mention was made about his having a part in the new venture, but he asked, "Can I assist the teacher, or do they both want lessons?"

"Fight it out between you," Toby said, and he walked up on the porch. "I'm starved," he said to Ma. "Anything to eat?"

"You'll find plenty left from dinner," Ma told him. "Hope you don't mind gettin' it for yourself. Got some apple tarts. You didn't eat none of them before you left awhile ago."

Steve didn't leave at once. He and Hank mumbled some plans about the guitar lessons. From the kitchen, Toby blurted out something—his mouth too full to say his words plainly enough to be understood. "He's tryin' to tell us that only one of the girls wants to learn to play," Hank said.

Steve offered to stay and help Toby and Hank with

their evening chores while Tom and Valinda went to sit awhile with a sick neighbor. With the work out of the way, the three boys sat on the porch again, enjoying the chill of the night, listening to the k-rump krr-rump and croak of the frogs in the pond near the Malcolm home. The crickets, chirping their songs, joined in the music. The three boys laughed and talked and played and sang.

But finally Steve strolled off down the moonlit road to his home, strumming his guitar as he went. The two brothers—Hank and Toby—went off to bed.

Just as Hank had told Susan he would do, he had quit school after finishing at the little brown schoolhouse. Toby had quit too. They helped Pa with the farm work. But there were times when even work on the farm slackened. Hank had not forgotten the lesson he was to give to the girl with the new guitar. One day when he found Toby working on some contraption at the toolshed, he announced that if Pa and Ma inquired about him, Toby could tell them he had gone to Maple Hill. Toby grunted his assent, but he seemed too busy just then to look up.

Hank started off down the road. He carried his guitar hung from his shoulder. Plink, plunk, plinkety-plank came from the strings of the instrument as Hank came to his friend Steve's house. Steve stood up, peering over a flowering shrub. Hank had come upon his friend, idling his time, apparently trying his hand at skipping stones across the smooth-swept ground that was the front yard of the Worth home.

"I thought I heard you coming," Steve said, with gladness expressing itself. "What's up?" he asked.

"Still want to go with me to Maple Hill?" Hank asked, ignoring the question. "This Miss what's-'er-name is going to have her first lesson today—that is, unless she refuses."

"Sure!" he answered quickly. "But, what're you gonna say when you get over there? You've never even seen 'em."

"Not backing out, are you?" Hank asked.

"I'm game if you are. I just wonder about barging in on somebody we don't even know, though."

Hank bent his knee and propped his foot backward against a tree. "Aw! Don't worry about not knowing them. It'll be all right, I'm sure." Hank was not exactly daring, but he was determined.

Turning a handspring, Steve landed upon the porch and ran inside for his own guitar, joining Hank, who had walked a few yards ahead of him by that time. It didn't take Steve long to catch up, and the two friends were on their way for a new adventure.

The boys strummed and hummed as they saun-tered into the small Maple Hill community. Hank had memorized directions to the house where this Vera and her sister lived, not far from Toby's friend Nancy. Hank had never had to worry about meeting people. Confidently he knocked on the door.

A girl opened to his knock.

"I'm Hank Malcolm, Toby's brother," he said. "This is my friend Steve. We heard you and your sister wanted to learn to play the guitar.

Only for a moment did the girl seem surprised; then, opening the door wider, she invited them in. "I'm Flora." The girl introduced herself.

Hank noticed another girl in the room, possibly that one was the Vera whom Toby had told him about. The parents were in the room as well.

The man stood up and welcomed Hank and Steve. "Come in, boys. Make yourself at home. Mrs. Korrel and I are happy to have you come."

"We saw a little boy on a bicycle out there." Steve spoke up and pointed outside.

"That was Jasper, our son," Mr. Korrel explained.

"You look mighty proud of 'im," Hank said.

"He's cute." Steve spoke again. "Don't blame you for being proud of 'im. We talked with him a little till he took off on that bicycle like a storm down the hill."

"That boy likes his bicycle," Mrs. Korrel added with a laugh.

Mr. Korrel seemed to like Hank from the beginning and fell into conversation with him right away. Hank learned the Korrels had come to Maple Hill from Larsen. Some thoughts popped into his head. His eyes wandered across the room, and he looked at the older girl—at Vera—and wondered if she was the girl who had called to him and Toby when they had peddled beef in Larsen several years ago. She'd asked to ride in their wagon.

Mrs. Korrel finally excused herself from the room, and soon Mr. Korrel found duties to which he had to attend. Somehow, then, the lesson on the guitar began. Although Flora was getting the lesson, Hank sensed that the other girl was showing him some interest. Vera talked only a little, but Hank noticed her staring at him.

Flora played the organ and sang well. She had played since her little toes could reach the pedals that had to be pumped to make the organ notes sound. With her good voice and Vera's not-too-discordant alto, combined with the two male voices, a nice quartet came about. And, besides a guitar lesson, there came this interest in singing as well.

Time slipped by quickly. Mrs. Korrell finally came in with a tempting refreshment, urging the boys to stay a little longer. It was dusk when the boys with their guitars left the Korrel home and started back to Oak Valley. On the way Hank and Steve discussed the afternoon with a degree of excitement sounding in their voices. As they talked, Steve vowed he was going to win Hank's pupil's interest.

"Suits me," Hank was quick to answer. "Not interested in no girl," he added. "But if I was, I see nothin' wrong with the other one—with Vera. You can have Flora if you like—if you can persuade her. But, no girl's gonna interest me."

"Oh, yes, some girl's gonna make you fall for her. And when you fall, well, you're gonna fall hard!"

Hank didn't answer. He just strummed some more on the guitar he was carrying.

It did not dawn on the boys that there was a similar conversation going on in the home they had just left. Flora kept trying to put her fingers on the strings of her guitar as Hank had shown her—trying hard to make the same chords on her guitar as she had made when he was helping her. Vera sat beside her. "Your teacher's a big fellow," she ventured. "And he sure is handsome!"

Flora kept her fingers in the position she had managed, but looked up. "Look out, my dear sister," she said. "I'll grant his appearance is rather captivating." Flora smiled and teased, "Are you about to—"

"You can have your teacher," Vera cut in, and rushed out of the room.

Syrup Making and Husking Bees

Fall was such a happy time around Oak Valley. The turning of the leaves to gold, purple, red, yellows, and brown made the woods pretty. Many were the interesting things to do in the country during the fall months—and all the other three seasons as well— though fall seemed the best time of the year.

On Sunday afternoons the community young people often spent time in the woods, reveling in the good things God gave for their enjoyment. They picked up hickory nuts, cracking them between smooth rocks. As they ate the nuts, they recalled happenings at school parties, or planned for things ahead.

It looked as if nature were having some special occasion, for she had pompously dressed herself. The sweet gum boasted a larger number of colors. In variation, it wore purple, gold, dark green, light green, red, yellow, and even brown, all at the same time. Hickory and poplar agreed on pure yellow-gold. Maple was splashed with gold and flame. There were oaks of various shades. Persimmon, bay, pine, and many other trees were native to the woods of Oak Valley.

A pleasant but tiring hike led the group up high on

the mountainside that overlooked a gurgling stream below. The young people found places to sit down for a rest and to continue the conversation. Some found logs for seats. Others just sat on the ground, which had a covering of clean fallen leaves, or bits of grass, now dying because summer was gone. Sawmen had felled a few trees nearby and left the stumps cut smooth, which made seats for a few.

"A glorious day!" exclaimed one of the girls, throwing both arms upward, as if to take in everything about them.

"Magnificent!" Toby Malcolm added.

And all agreed. It was wonderful to live in Oak Valley. It was wonderful to be young and alive!

Monday morning, early, found the two Malcolm boys in the sugarcane patch. There were workers in other patches in the neighborhood. The swordlike leaves were stripped from the bluish-purple stalks. Broken-off fodder lay in the furrows, leaving patches of cane that, though earlier in the day looked like jungles, now were patches of bare stalks, resembling tropical palms; for the top leaves were left to be broken off when the stalks would be cut down. When the stalks were cut and the tops broken off, the cane could be loaded on wagons and hauled to the mill. By night a few loads had reached the site where cane syrup would be made. Toby and Hank got one load there the first day, but it was nearly dark when they did.

"Put your pile over yonder." These words came from the man who was in charge. A place was designated for each farmer. Not enough cane arrived the first day to start the grinding and cooking; so the copper pan was not set up, nor a fire started in the furnace that day. It was the third day before the syrup-making really began.

A party had been planned for the first night that the mill was in full operation. All the young people expressed readiness—the older ones too. No clouds showed to mar the hope of a moonlight night. Dusk found groups of young people and parents appearing in the clearing in the woods from several directions.

Pretty patterns showed at the end of the thicket as the moon's rays beamed down, slipping between the branches. A little over the hill, down in a hollow near the stream, stood the great furnace. The belches of smoke were mixed with flames at the top of the chimney. Then, thinning, the smoke reached high and spread wide overhead. In front of the furnace stood a man with a big ladle in his hand.

Close by, another man sat at the grinding mill, where the stalks were poked in—going in whole but coming out on the other side pressed thin and flat. The juice from the pressing apparatus found its way into a trough and then into a tub, over which a white cloth had been stretched to strain pieces of trash.

The mill workmen showed no displeasure at the crowds that came around while they were working. From appearances, there would be a gay time offered by the party makers. The girls had brought big supplies of fudge, popped corn, and panfuls of roasted peanuts. One of the boys thought of marshmallows, and had brought them to be roasted from long sticks that could reach the coals in the furnace. There would be games, and someone would tell a story.

Hank looked around to see if the Korrel girls were at the party. He tried to casually ask different ones about the Korrels, but he was informed each time that they were different. "Got some funny idea about everything!"

Hank talked to Steve about it.

"I don't know," Steve answered. "That Flora and Vera seemed all right to me when we was over there."

One crisp November morning Tom Malcolm called, "You 'wake boys?" He opened the door a crack to the room where Hank and Toby slept. But Pa did not get an answer.

The two boys appeared to be still asleep. Since Toby had not answered, and Pa was still waiting, Hank grunted out, "Why can't a fellow sleep when it's Thanksgiving?"

But, when Pa said, "Your Ma and me's decided that we'd give a corn husking tonight," four feet hit the floor at the same time, and that many legs jumped into jeans. Then Pa's voice died away as he said, "They's lots to get done," for he was walking down the hall back to the kitchen to join Ma and Susan who had returned home for the Thanksgiving holiday season.

"Is breakfast ready, Ma?" Hank wanted to know. He was ready, now, to get busy.

"Bring it on," Toby called to Susan, as he dropped himself on the bench beside his brother, who had beat him to the table.

"Get up and go wash your hands before you come to the table." Susan acted bossy. Then she set a plate of hot biscuits on and some golden brown homemade bread.

Every face expressed smiles at the table. It was always that way when something interesting was

81

happening. With breakfast over, each one went to his appointed duty.

"Since Toby's not as strong," Pa said, "he should ride around the community and give the invitation to the bee."

Toby made no arguments about that, and Hank certainly had no objection, for Hank knew it was the reasonable thing to do. He and Pa would get the poles hauled from the woods, and when Toby got back, he could help with the sawing.

The old horse, Kate, was no longer with the family; so Maud was saddled, and Toby rode horseback. It was late in the morning before he returned. He came into the drive, whistling. "Believe everybody'll turn out," he announced. "Not a one refused."

"Didn't expect 'em to, did you?" Hank blurted out, glad, though, for Toby's report. Hank was all full of expectation for the party.

The poles for firewood had been unloaded by the sawhorse. "You take a break," Toby suggested to Pa. "Me and Hank can saw, now that I'm back—rested and rarin' to go."

Hank sanctioned the suggestion. And Toby took hold of the end of the saw opposite his brother.

"I ain't a bit tired," Pa said. "But I'll step to the house and fetch us some water. That'll put us fit; and while you saw, I'll stack the sawed wood. We can take turns at pulling the saw. It won't take us too long, that-a-way."

When Pa passed through the kitchen door, going inside, odors of good things cooking came out, reaching the noses of the two at the crosscut saw. "I bet Ma's making 'lasses cookies for tonight," Hank guessed.

"And Susan'll roast good, crisp, brown peanuts, as usual," Toby added.

"That Susan knows just how to parch 'em," Hank said. "She can beat Ma on that."

"Reckon what kind of cook Sally Boutwell'll be?" Toby teased. Though Hank did not look, he felt the thrusting look of his brother, knowing he was poking fun at him—just because he didn't have much use for girls.

"Mix a little more work with your talkin'," Pa suggested as he returned. The saw began to buzz again—and a little faster. Hank pulled at one end, then Toby pulled back the other way, making the saw sink the sharp teeth deep into the wood, eating its way through, until a fire-length log fell to the ground for Pa to stack.

When time came for the noon meal, because the men were so nearly through with the wood cutting, they did not quit to eat at the regular time, preferring to finish the job. After dinner there were other things to do before time for the guests to arrive. One end of the barn floor was swept clean, and seats were improvised by standing short blocks of wood on end and placing thick pieces of lumber on them. A homemade table sat in the middle of one end of the floor, where refreshements could be served during the evening.

The hours passed. The many jobs were about done, and so was the day. The sun sank sleepily—not clear, but dusky red. A few clouds hung about. Tonight the moon would not rise until long after all the huskers had gone home and would be in bed. Although a moonlit night makes a party more delightful sometimes, it would not be necessary tonight; for the party would be inside the barn, and there would be several kerosene lanterns hanging from the barn's overhead joists to give light.

Ma called to Hank from the back door. She was about to tell him, he knew, to hurry with the milking. He laughed because she did not have to tell him. He was already going to the house with the pail brimful of milk. He had slipped out with the milk bucket and had milked so fast that the fresh, warm milk had beat up into a foam on top, and was actually running over the sides. "Old Bossy just kep givin' milk," he said, "and me in a hurry to get through." Hank chuckled and handed the pail of milk to his mother.

The supper meal was cut short. No one was hungry. Hank wiped the dishes for Susan. Pa shaved, and Ma put on a fresh dress. Toby was at the front, ready to receive the guests. And when there was a sound of mingled voices and laughter outside, Susan slammed the last dish out onto the table for Hank to wipe and put away, then dashed the pan of water out on the backyard. Hank half wiped the dish and threw the dish towel at a nail on the wall, where, fortunately, it caught by the crocheted edge. The two scooted, anxious to greet the first arrivals even though Toby was there to welcome them.

Hank kept straining to see someone. But with the arrival of each guest he sighed and became less and less happy.

People gathered fast and went directly to the barn. "Work first—then play!" came from Mr. Thorne, when people found places to sit. He was acting as master of ceremonies, for Pa had asked him to. Husks began to fly to the husk bin; and the big, well-formed ears of corn fell into another bin. The husking began with a storm. Old and young worked to get the job finished. A party was coming up!

At the proper time, Ma went to the kitchen. When she returned, she brought a kettleful of candied molasses, ready for the taffy pull. Two at a time took handfuls of the still-warm sticky substance and pulled it into ropes and refolded it until it was nearly white, and brittle. Each couple vied with the others to see who could end up with the prettiest and crispest stick of candy.

Toby and Mable won the taffy prize. Another prize went to Peter Thorne for bobbing for apples. There were other games with prizes. Cookies and peanuts were not forgotten. Time seemed to hurry, as if it could not wait to make the evening late. But Mr. Thorne asked Pa if they might have a little more time. With Pa's agreement to his request, he called out, "Come on, boys, with your guitars." Hank and Steve, having their instruments with them, chorded a little, then struck up a tune. No one had to be urged to sing with the music. That is, no one but Hank. He played his guitar halfheartedly, but he didn't sing with the others. Something seemed to be missing at the husking party.

Susan and Sally sat near the music makers and joined heartily with the crowd as all sang. Steve didn't have to tell that he was flattered to have Susan near him—it showed. It did not matter to Hank who sat with him. But it surely seemed to matter to Sally. But, since Sally was a jolly type, Hank tried to act glad for her company.

The singing slowed a little. One here and there began to call out to Pa to dance a jig. "Pa doesn't like to show off," Hank whispered to Steve. He turned to

Sally as he finished that statement to give her notice as he spoke.

"He's won prizes for his dancing." Sally spoke, and she joined in the applause that was urging Pa.

After such urgent applause, Pa got up, grinning from ear to ear.

"Pa enjoys it." His son with the guitar added this to what he had said to Steve and Sally.

When Pa began, the floor began to shake violently. Everyone screamed, adding to the noise. Ma was proud of her man. It showed on her face because of the smile. But Ma never took much part in dancing. After a buck dance or two, and Pa had shown the crowd that he could almost reach the top of the door casing with his toes, he sat down and blew as if out of breath.

Yawns from one here and there made the crowd realize it was time to go home. Some of the little ones had gone to sleep and were lying on pallets on the floor. Mothers woke them, and the party broke. A jolly crowd bade the Malcolm family goodnight and thanked them for the enjoyable time at the party.

Chattering voices died away outside as guests made their several ways to their own homes.

The Big-Tent Meetings

The winter had been mighty long. Susan had returned to college. Tom and Valinda Malcolm expressed their feelings, adding, "With you boys goin' to Maple Hill so much, it makes Susan's bein' away worse."

But winter did not last always. It never does. The cold days come, and then they have a way of disappearing into spring. And, the coming of this spring would bring Susan home again. The warm days made Oak Valley take on a dress of tender new leaves and buds, as well as blossoms here and there. Songbirds, too, announced another glorious season was coming. Pa and Ma went about the place with steps more lively, and a tune could be heard as Ma worked. Pa whistled more than usual also. Then things about the farm began to take on shape for a new crop. Now work held the boys at home except on Sundays.

Miles away a homesick girl lay awake some at night, listening to train whistles as the big engines, with cars rolling behind, thundered over the tracks not far from the college dormitory. "I'll soon be riding in one of those cinder-filled cars toward home," Susan told herself. "I've been away from my family too long." She choked as she thought of how good it would be to have her own people around her again. In spite of her separation from the family, however, winter had passed fast enough, because she had studied hard and had made new acquaintances. But, as the time drew near, she grew more anxious. "I wonder if they've bought an automobile yet." She thought, and then added, "I don't guess they have. Their letters would surely tell that if they had. I wonder if Toby's still interested in Nancy."

Time came when there was only one week before Susan would leave for home. That day was a Wednesday. Thursday was filled with tests, Friday about the same. Then the weekend came. Next Monday all Susan's things were packed, and Tuesday she waited. On Wednesday she bade farewell to college friends. Amidst the smiles of joy there were the tears of sadness at parting from friends.

The train left on time, but it would stop at every crossing before arriving at Larsen. However, even with the many stops the time rolled on, as did the train, and at last it arrived at the little station near her home.

"I never knew I would miss all of you so much," Susan greeted her brothers Toby and Hank when they rushed up to her. They had come in the carriage to meet the train. Anxious to get home, she climbed in the front seat between the boys. "How long will it take to drive to Oak Valley—and to Pa and Ma?" She chuckled.

There were so many new things to talk about. Susan learned about the new acquaintances of the boys, and the happenings in general. And she herself had a big surprise for the family—the announcement of her engagement to Doctor Hosea's son, Tim. It was a fulfillment of Pa's prediction of a few months ago, that "some man'll want her." And although it was not a complete surprise to her folks, they still showed the proper amount of excitement and elation.

"I know he was off to medical college," Pa stated.

"You mean you've given Steve Worth the cold shoulder?" Toby asked her.

"Looks like I don't have to." Susan laughed. "I hear he's got interests in Maple Hill. How does it happen that the three of you have left Oak Valley girls in pursuit of Maple Hill beauties?"

"Uh—uh." Hank started.

"Don't deny it, young man," Toby broke in. "You've fell at last. Steve's been tellin' you you'd do it." Then Toby looked toward Susan. "He's fell for Vera."

"Who's Vera?" Susan wanted to know.

Although Tom and Valinda had heard of Vera Korrel and that she was one of those queer Seventh-day Adventists, and they were aware of the get-togethers at Maple Hill, this statement of Toby's seemed to strike an unfavorable chord with both of them.

"Not really! Hank ain't fell for no girl!" Ma spoke up. "She's got that queer religion."

"Don't worry about Hank, Ma," Susan comforted. "You know he has never had a serious thought about any girl. He'll be all right." Being in love herself, Susan really felt for her young brother's rights in that matter. Of course, she knew counsel was good. But she wondered why religion should make the difference—and more so since they were making no particular profession themselves.

Toby said no more. Hank found business elsewhere, and the subject died.

"Hank's mighty settled," Pa said as the boys left him and Ma alone with Susan. "I hope he won't get mixed up wrong."

The sun continued to sink lower and lower. The sky reddened, and then the colors of purple and gold mingled with the red. Susan sat on the porch with Ma and Pa. They watched the sky and exclaimed over its beauty. Susan talked about her days at college and her engagement to Dr. Hosea's son.

Pa reached over and took Ma's hand in his, and they smiled at each other as Susan talked on.

The next day Toby asked Ma and Pa if he and Hank could use the buggy that evening. "There's some tent meetings beginning over in Larsen," he said. "We thought we'd go over this evening."

"Oh, I'd like to go with you," Susan said.

"Well, what dya' think, Ma? Shall we let 'em have the buggy?" Pa asked.

Ma nodded. "I don't make no mind. It'd be good for the young uns to go."

In privacy Ma told Pa that she hoped Hank might find new interest there and forget about Vera Korrel. "I wonder who's holdin' the meetings. I s'pose they's religious meetings. Had you heerd the church was goin' to hold a revival? Did Brother Thrasher tell ya about that?"

Pa shook his head.

Susan and Hank and Toby and Steve Worth drove in the buggy to the edge of Larsen, where a big tent had been set up. People were thronging into the place. Much to Susan's surprise she found Hank and Toby had arranged to meet Nancy Brooks and the two

Korrel girls there. Of course, she already knew Nancy. She liked Vera and Flora Korrel right away. They all sat near the front of the tent, and all joined in the singing.

Susan watched Hank, who sat on the far end of the bench beside Vera. He seemed to be drinking in every word the preacher said. When the meeting closed, he seemed more quiet than usual as the group of young folks walked to the place where they had left the buggy. Flora, Vera, and Nancy said good night and then strolled off toward their homes.

"I like those girls," Susan said. "Flora doesn't seem very interested in Steve. That'll break up soon," she said when they had dropped Steve off at his place. "I like Vera," she went on to say. "I think, Hank, you've made a good choice."

Hank mumbled, "I—I—ain't worthy of her."

Susan shook her head and smiled at her brother. "Nonsense! You're worthy of the best, brother."

"Nancy 'n me'll be hitched before many weeks," Toby announced, and he grinned broadly.

"What? You don't mean you're really that serious, do you?" Susan asked.

"Yep!" Toby replied.

"Have you told Ma and Pa?" Susan wanted to know as they drove up to the house and saw Ma and Pa seated on the porch.

"Nope!" Toby answered. "Not yet. I'll do it when I guess it's best."

Susan seemed to sense that Ma and Pa might object to their attending the tent meetings if they knew the meetings were being held by Seventh-day Adventists. However, when Pa asked about the preaching, Susan remembered that the preacher had talked about the strange animals in the book of Daniel, and reckoned that if Brother Thrasher would learn the Bible as the preacher at the big tent, Pa would have to read up a lot to get ahead of Brother Thrasher. Without mentioning the name of the preacher or to what church he belonged, Susan began to tell Ma and Pa some of the things the preacher had said about Daniel and the animals he mentioned.

"Never did understand that book of Daniel," Pa said. "Guess I'll have to study up on it. Sounds real interestin'."

The Holy Spirit Speaks

Susan managed frequent visits to the big tent with the younger Malcolms. For Susan and Toby it was a chance to "get together" with the young people of the communities around. But it was different for Hank. There was a drawing upon his heart that he had never felt before. Hank was hearing words of truth. Of course he was glad to be with Vera on those nights when his sister and brother and he could go to the meetings, but even more important to him were the words he heard from the Bible and the occasional words from Vera on Bible subjects. These things became fixed in his mind.

Hank found himself wondering what it would mean if he should make such a life as Vera's a part of his own. The more he thought about it, the more he felt something pulling at him. He remembered the time when he and Toby sold beef from house to house. He remembered the little girl giggling and calling to them to let her ride in the wagon. Her family did not eat meat, and they went to church on Saturday; but now, to him, the girl, Vera, was the most wonderful girl he had ever known. Vera had shown him reasons for her beliefs. Now, words cited from Scriptures at the big tent were impressing him—were pricking his heart. To accept this new way of life would mean a big change for him. What would Pa and Ma say about it? Things seemed to be forming a difficult situation for Hank. Yet he did not feel he could ignore the something that seemed to be speaking to him.

"Why?" Hank questioned himself. "Why should I let this get me down? I have never gone to church to amount to much. I get along all right. I ain't no bad guy, and maybe I still don't need to belong to some group of people just because they are following what is laid down in the Bible."

Hank's very last words answered the question he was putting to himself. "Following what is laid down in the Bible," he repeated to himself. "Yes, that is the reason I should belong to that group of people." Then the other side of the argument presented itself again. "What would Pa and Ma think? What would they say? They don't like the mention of Seventh-day Adventists—don't even want me to be seein' Vera." All these things troubled Hank, whose respect for his parents was very strong.

Once again duties in the field occupied the time of the Malcolm young men and Pa. But the duties, though helping, did not completely take away Hank's troubled thoughts. Pa and Ma talked with each other about Hank's late behavior.

"Oh, well," Pa said. "Boys are gonna go over 'fool's hill,' and then when they get over it, all their foolish ideas vanish."

Sometimes Hank was himself again. When he and Toby got to telling tales of their former escapades, they laughed. While they were hoeing near the old dinkey rail track, they spoke of the time when Hank had slipped away and had taken the ride on the dinkey train. Hank told Toby and Pa, "That was a fine old man, that Mr. Kelley. He might seem rough, bein' big and husky and doin' that kind of work. I found him a likable fellow. He didn't have any teeth, and when he chewed his tobacco, his chin and nose almost met." Pa and Toby and he laughed as he reminisced.

Without any urging from Pa and Toby, Hank went on about Mr. Kelley. "He wore an old felt hat—broadbrim—turned up in the front and down in the back. Sometimes as he watched his work on the road, he would take a drink of coffee that was kept hot on the engine."

"Who was the other man?" Toby asked—"the fireman?"

"That was Mr. Galliger," Hank answered. "When he saw the steam gettin' low, he threw another chunk of wood in the furnace."

"Did you ever get to talk with the Mr. Kelley and Mr. Galliger?" That was Pa's question.

"Oh, yes, when they stopped to fire up," Hank remembered. "And you know," he went on, enjoying the remembrance of the day, "I remember that Mr. Galliger would sometimes mention the Korrel family. He seemed to know them. Think he worked some with Mr. Korrel." Then Hank hushed quickly. He was bordering on a subject that might not be of interest to Pa. Besides, it brought that urging feeling that he had been having since he had been seeing Vera Korrel. It reminded him too, of the words the preacher at the big tent had spoken: "We ought to obey God rather then man."

"Although I have never read the Good Book myself,

I can't help but believe that we should obey its words," Hank thought quietly.

There would be only one more week of the meetings held in the big tent in Larsen. Perhaps after the meetings he would not be so troubled.

The services at the big tent had meant more than a way to spend lonely evenings, Hank knew. His visits with Vera and her family had impressed him more and more with the importance of the truths of the Bible. At the tent meetings he had listened to sermons that had made the truths more clear. Now he felt deeply convicted. He needed, yes, he wanted a change in his life. The Holy Spirit spoke to him in a quiet but forceful voice. Hank had a problem. Ma and Pa would certainly oppose him in a decision such as he felt convicted he should make. "But why?" he pondered, "They have never expressed reasons other than that those Saturday keepers seem strange and mixed up. They don't go to any particular church themselves. Pa always reads the Bible and calls it the 'Good Book.' "

Hank wished he could talk with Ma and Pa about the tent services. But Susan and Toby had said over and over that they had better say nothing about those meetings or they might not be allowed to go. But Hank also knew that Susan and Toby did not really feel concerned about what they were hearing at the meetings.

That evening at the supper table Hank was startled when Toby blurted out, "This Friday night, and then—then—" he seemed embarrassed and stopped in midsentence.

"Then what?" Susan asked.

"Then—then—" he began and stopped as if searching for help. Suddenly he added hurriedly, "I guess we'll have to miss a night or two of the meetings next week. If Ma and Pa'll let us have the buggy for tonight and Sunday night—"

Susan interrupted. "Toby, you know the meetings will end on Friday night.

"Sure you young uns can have the buggy this week," Pa agreed. "Meetin's, good meetin's, never hurt no one."

Friday came all too soon to suit Hank. At the close of the meeting at the tent Susan, Hank, and Toby, along with Steve Worth, stood in a circle with Nancy, Vera, and Flora. Toby seemed very reluctant to break up the group for the evening. At last, jingling the coins in his pocket, he suggested they all go to the ice-cream store down on the corner. "I'll buy us all some ice cream!"

"Good idea. I'll pitch in with some coins too. Where's our little mascot?" Steve Worth spoke up.

"You mean Jasper? Here he is," Nancy laughed as the youngest member of the Korrel family came running to join the group.

"You'll have to excuse us," Flora Korrel took Jasper's hand.

"Could we wait to have the treat another time?" Vera asked. "You know, as Seventh-day Adventists we don't do things like that on Friday night. That's something we can do any other night of the week, but Friday is special. It's the beginning of the Sabbath and—"

"What else don't you do—" Steve broke in. "We knowed you don't work nor buy on Saturday because it's Sabbath, but Friday night too?"

No one spoke for a moment.

"This is too much!" Steve spoke up again. "Saturday keepers and Friday night too!"

"You see," Vera explained, "the Sabbath begins at sundown on Friday evening, and ends at sundown on Saturday. Those hours are special hours set apart by God as holy time."

The group listened. After a pause Nancy shrugged. "Beats me!"

"Aw, come on," Toby looked from one girl to another. "I thought a day began at midnight."

Jasper looked straight at Toby. "My Pa says that it is told in Genesis—right in the beginning of the story of Creation—that the evening comes first before the daylight time. It takes the evening and the morning, the Bible says, to make a day. My Pa says that means a night and a day makes twenty-four hours, and the night comes first."

Everyone laughed a little at Jasper's explanation. Flora gave her little brother a big hug.

Hank had been listening intently to every word of the conversation. Now he spoke up, shifting his weight from one foot to the other. "Of course we won't go tonight. Let's wait until one night next week."

That night when Hank went to bed, he could not seem to fall asleep. He turned and tossed, and at last he slipped out of bed. Quietly he tiptoed down the hall past Susan's room and beyond where Ma and Pa slept. Cautiously, he opened the side door and slipped out onto the porch.

"Why am I so troubled?" he asked himself. "Why should I be troubled about obeying God's word? Of course I don't want to cause confusion in the home. If only Ma and Pa wouldn't feel as they do about this strange religion."

Hank looked up into the starry sky as if searching for an answer. He was doubly troubled, for there was also the thought of the conflict that would arise should he marry Vera. He knew now he would never be happy without her. And he knew that they would never be truly happy if he led such a different life from her way. Vera seemed to be as interested in him as he was in her. Their caring had sort of been unspoken between them. But would she—? He stopped thinking these thoughts.

"I know God is speaking to me," he said at last. "I've heard of the Holy Spirit—how it works. I don't know how to pray, but I can talk to God, I guess. I gotta talk to Him." The boy slipped from the stool where he sat. He went to his knees, something pressing inside of him. "I am goin' to be different. I'm goin' to keep the Sabbath that I have learned about. God, help me," was his silent prayer.

The heaviness in Hank's heart seemed to lighten. Now, a new Hank retraced his steps to the bedroom, where he joined his brother in peaceful slumber. His decision was made. But his parents had to be faced.

Double Conflict

Hank decided to face the issue and have a talk with Pa. No matter, he would serve God—that he had decided. If Pa and Ma were going to object to the girl of his choice, it would pose another big problem for him; for he had much respect for his parents. He wanted to please them. If he could convince his father that Vera was a fine girl, Pa could persuade Ma. In case they would not be convinced, he would have to consider carefully the next step. What should he do? Then there was another problem: Did Vera care for him as much as he cared for her? Hank would not want to hurt Vera. This was the greatest trouble that had come to his young mind. He loved his family. And yet, his first love of a girl had taken hold upon him.

In the field the day he decided to talk with Pa, Hank chopped vigorously at first, ridding the cotton rows of their weeds; yet his thoughts were on other things. He could feel that Pa was watching him.

"Son," Mr. Malcolm finally spoke, almost startling the dreamy one before he had had time to approach his Pa on the subject.

Hank stopped hoeing and looked over at Pa, who stood, one field shoe on top of the other and both hands clutching the top of his hoe handle.

"Er—uh, Son," the older man spoke again. "Somethin's botherin' you. You ain't keepin' up with yer pa."

Hank saw that his father was trying to bring him around to the very conversation that he, himself, had wanted to open. "Pa," he said in response, "I reckon I'm thinkin' harder'n I'm workin'." He paused and looked off into space as if searching for words—the right words.

"Pa," he started again. "What would you think if I married Vera. I don't *have* to go to her church. But, even if I did, I don't go to church anywhere else. Looks like it would be better'n not goin' at all." Then, in a quiet but firm tone, he added, "But I want to be a Seventh-day Adventist myself."

Complete silence followed Hank's statement. Hank noticed that his Pa looked mighty troubled. For a moment his hands trembled as they clutched the top of his hoe. However, since Pa never spoke harsh words to his children, Hank knew he would not do that now. Still, he waited to hear his father's reaction.

At last Pa said in a very quiet voice, "That girl's used to more'n you can offer her, my boy."

That matter had in no way been forgotten by Hank. "The heifers you give to both me and Toby will be puttin' Jersey 'gold' in the bank before long." Hank knew that the talk of the calves was as music to the ears of Mr. Malcolm.

"Son, save some of the heifers—the finer ones—to build up your herd," Pa advised. He grunted as if to say a little more about the calves, but he dropped his hoe by the side of the row and, looking back toward Hank, said, "I've got to go see yer ma a minute. You can finish your row and go to the shade awhile. Go to the spring yonder and get a cool drink."

Hank watched his father parting the cotton plants carefully as he passed among them crossing the rows on his way to the house. "Pa's gonna talk to Ma about what I said. I was hoping he could talk with me, and I could persuade him, then he might make Ma have less opposition." He would go to the spring. First he looked up the row to view his work. When he did, he saw—not freshly stirred dirt, nor grass wilting beside the lush growth of cotton stalks but a woman coming toward him from across the field.

"Vera!" Hank exclaimed. "How did you get here?"

Vera laughed and brushed loose strands of hair from her face. "Jostling through these rows of cotton tousles one's hair."

"How'd you know how to find me? Or, were you looking for me?"

"I asked Mrs. Malcolm." The girl took off a slipper as she took hold of Hank's hoe handle to balance herself. She emptied the slipper of the dirt that had gotten in, then she replaced the shoe. As she looked up at Hank, her face reddened. Hank thought she must be embarrassed because she had come to the field to see him. He wanted to take hold of the hand still holding his hoe handle, but he didn't. There was yet an issue involved.

"Want a job?" Hank asked, wondering how Vera felt toward a man who had farmed all his life. Her smile made him feel it did not matter to her if he was a farm boy. "I was just starting to the spring for a drink," Hank told his visitor. "Come along. You may be thirsty after a long walk." Hank led the way.

A willow at the spring made shade for them as Vera told Hank her mission over to Oak Valley, and to the field to see him. "I'm going away," she said. "I'll be gone for several months. I'm going to some temporary work in the city." She told him too that Flora was going away for nurses' training.

As Vera told him these things, dozens of things ran through his already heavy mind. He would miss the only girl he had ever loved. She might find another man and forget him. How much more could he take? But he would not tell her now how he felt.

The girl rose to go. It was not easy for Hank to let her leave. He could not refrain from taking her hand, but she drew away. "I'll see you when I come back." That was her promise as she left Hank standing there in the shade of the willows by the spring. She looked back and waved and then disappeared from Hank's sight.

The girl had a battle to fight too. Although she was not aware of the struggle Hank was experiencing, she did know that she had a decision of her own to make. Vera knew that she, a Christian girl, should not have allowed herself to become so friendly with one not of her faith. "I have made a mistake," she said, weeping as she went on her way toward the road that would take her back to Maple Hill. "I am in love with Hank," she acknowledged. "And, I find myself wanting to hold onto him. I don't want to break our friendship now. He wants me too. I know he does. What a mistake I have made!"

The road was long ahead of Vera—several miles. Walking the miles alone, she would have time to think. "I must not. I must not go on," she told herself and shed some more tears. "It's enough for me to be hurt, but I hate to hurt him. I should not have done it, and now I am having to be punished. God has been so good to me—and is to those who obey Him. I have so much enjoyed my Christian experience. But—but!"

Vera remembered that that very morning God had answered prayers that the way be opened for Flora to go for nurses' training. "He never fails us when we, in Christian faith, pray."

Vera sat beside the road to rest. She was not accustomed to so much walking. It was good to be alone to think over the problem that was causing her so great mental stress at the present. The girl wiped her face with a dainty handkerchief. She fanned herself with the bottom of her long skirt. "Going over to the field where Hank was at work made me feel a little nearer to him." She plucked at a blade of sedge grass and then broke a stalk of it, chewing at the stem. The juice tasted sweet, and the bit of moisture quenched her thirst somewhat.

"Hank is so like a Christian, so like an Adventist," the girl mused. "It was just too easy for me to go this far and get involved with him to the point of caring."

As Vera still sat, she recalled the day when her father had bought a little book from a salesman passing by. At the time she had not known that it was called *Christian Sabbath*, for her father and mother did not allow her and Flora to see the book until they, themselves, had read it and weighed its contents. Of course Jasper could not read at the time, and it did not matter if he saw the book. "How curious I was," Vera recollected. "I wanted to know what was in that book. Then, when my parents talked the matter over with the family, we decided to keep the seventh-day Sabbath, though we had never heard of a group of people who worshiped on that day."

As the girl reminisced, the story continued to play itself on her mental stage. Soon they had learned of a church not too distant, and had begun to attend. She smiled as she remembered little Jasper standing on a chair beside the superintendent and repeating several memory verses at a time. "He had a good memory—learned the Scripture verses easier than Flora and I did," she said aloud, laughing as she thought of her little brother lisping out the Bible verses.

Suddenly realizing she was talking to herself, she said, "Oh well, who cares? I'm not talking to me. I'm talking to you creatures flying about overhead." She looked up at the branches reaching over her almost across the road. She could see familiar spots ahead that told her she would soon be home.

Serious thoughts came again. "I cannot risk confusion in my life—nor maybe disruption to Hank's family. I must obey the commands of the Bible."

Then, thoughts of the temporary job waiting for her hastened to ease the hurt in her heart. But it was a hurt that would be hard to erase.

Double or Nothin'

It was a Tuesday morning late in the summer. Soon there would be a stir on the Malcolm farm again, for harvesttime would begin. Susan would be going back to her second year at college and would be busy with her studies. Hank seemed like his natural self since Vera had gone, but he spent a lot of time reading the Bible, especially on Saturdays.

The Malcolm five were gathered about the breakfast table, chatting merrily. Toby thought this a good time to make his proposal to Pa and Ma. He cleared his throat. "Ma," he began, "had you and Pa heard there is to be a singing in the Maple Hill church next Sunday?" He looked toward Hank, then toward Susan, hoping one of them would help him out. But neither said a word. This was Toby's deal; and if no one else said anything, he would have to go ahead with it.

"That ought to please me and your pa," Mrs. Malcolm spoke. "We ain't been out to no singing nor to church, either, lately. We ought to get out more'n we do." She looked in Pa's direction.

"It'll be a good time to wear your new dress," was Pa's comment. That was all the answer that Toby needed.

Plans began to take shape at once. Baskets of fine

foods would be prepared. The carriage wooden wheels would be wetted to make them swell and fit tight to the outer iron rim. This would be done at the creek. Jokes were told now and then, keeping up a merry spirit. As usual, Toby had a tale or joke to tell for laughs. Late in the week he got the attention of the family, one evening, when he started out with one of his stories.

"Last Sunday at church—" Toby started, then he explained that he had gone to church with Nancy. "The collection plate was passed. When the deacon came to Uncle Henry, he pulled out a twenty-dollar bill and asked for change." Toby saw that Ma was watching him. He didn't look in Pa's direction. "Of course there wasn't half that much on the collection plate; so Uncle Henry just said, 'You'll have to pass me up this time, and I'll give double—or nothin'—next time.'"

"Watch what you're sayin'." Pa chided. And Ma told Toby that he should tell it straight or not tell it at all.

"Well, maybe he didn't add the words 'or nothin',' but from the way he squirmed and because he does the same thing all the time, he musta meant it."

When Sunday morning came, it broke clear as any August day. "Yippee!" Toby yelled. He brought a fresh bucket of water from the spring and set it heavily on the shelf, causing a slosh that spilled down the front of his jeans and wet the boards of the porch floor. Pouring a gourdful into the basin, he washed his hands and splashed some of the refreshing water onto his face.

When Toby came to the breakfast table, he commented on the nice day for the singing at Maple Hill. Pa seemed to look at him kind of strange, he thought. He wondered if Pa was guessing that something was up.

Hank said he wondered if Aunt Molly Hines would be there. If she were, he guessed she'd have a platter of fried eggs for the picnic lunch.

Toby laughed at Hank's remark but seemed rather preoccupied.

"What's got into you?" Ma asked.

"Nothin'! Nothing'!" Toby assured her.

As soon as the breakfast was finished, the family began to make ready for the trip to Uncle Henry's church. Pa and Ma and Susan would go in the buggy. Toby and Hank would walk, taking the shortcut. Soon the family was on the way.

At the church there was a stir. Conversation was a-buzz. Old friends were glad, plainly, to see each other again and had to exchange tales common to them. The one who had been elected to be chairman rapped a gavel on the desk to call the assembly to order. People quickly found seats.

Tom and Valinda sat near the middle of the church. Mrs. Malcolm looked over the crowd. "I'm curious to know if there are many here that I know—wonder if Henry and Violet are here." She punched Pa in the side with her elbow. "I see Miss Lucy Short. She had to wear that fascinator under her Sunday hat—and it's August!" Pa tried to quiet Ma. But then she whispered a little louder. "Yonder's Violet. She's up closer to the front."

The singing began, music sounding through the windows and wafting on the air for a long distance. The way the people sang one would guess that all of them were enjoying it. A short sermon finished out the morning; then it came time for the baskets of food to be spread.

There were stews, bakings, salads, and other foods that would tempt hungry folk. A few had brought lemonade. Then, what eating and drinking and talking! Many expressed their feelings that the noon hour had been all too short. The bell rang for the crowd to reassemble.

Returning to the church, Pa pointed. "Look, Ma, Toby and Nancy's sittin' right on the front bench."

Ma looked that way. "They ain't singers. Nancy's mighty dressed up," Ma commented.

"No more'n you. And you look fine." Pa looked fondly at Ma. "I promised you years ago that I'd dress you up fine when I could sell enough cotton and calves—more than we actually needed for other things." Then Pa added, "You look real pretty."

Ma smiled coquettishly. But the many years of hard work, since the time Pa had promised her that, had told tales of age on Valinda's face. Age doesn't wait for cotton to be picked nor calves to grow.

The moderator rapped his gavel. The noisy crowd quieted somewhat. The man at the rostrum spoke. "I would like to have your attention, please," he said. "The directors for the afternoon will be announced later—in just a little. But right now we have something special. Well, that is—or—" he stammered. "There's to be a—a surprise."

Susan nudged Hank. "Sit up straight and watch!" she whispered. "It's about to happen."

The moderator sat down. The word *surprise* does something to people, and quietness reigned throughout the room. The preacher came and took the moderator's place behind the pulpit.

"Already had a sermon," Ma whispered.

The preacher did not begin speaking. He stood gazing out into the audience. Then two young people began to approach him. Ma sat up on the edge of her seat. "It's Toby—"

And Pa added, "and Nancy."

When the two stopped in front of the pulpit, the minister began to speak some words in soft tones— words such as had been heard spoken to couples such as Toby and Nancy since ages back. Then he finished his remarks by saying, "I now pronounce you husband and wife."

Pa and Ma paled. Ma drew a pretty handkerchief from her handbag and wiped a falling tear from one cheek, then the other. Pa's rough hand smeared moisture across his face. He reached over and took the trembling hand that lay in Ma's lap and pressed it gently.

At home that evening, Hank said, "Maybe with Uncle Henry it's 'double or nothin',' but for Toby, he musta thought he was nothin' unless he could double his life with Nancy's."

"Actually, I'm glad he did," Susan said. "Nancy'll be a good 'sidekick' for our brother."

Pa and Ma were silent. The marriage of their middle child had been a big surprise.

Uncle Henry's Visit

Susan returned to college. Toby and Nancy were married, and Hank had not heard from Vera for some time. He would have been very lonely had it not been for Steve. The two close friends sat side by side on the steps of the front porch one afternoon.

"I miss Flora—liked her a lot," Steve broke the silence.

"Looks like you've taken to Sally. She's a nice girl—pretty, too." Hank laughed.

"You don't feel I'm takin' your girl away from you?" Steve asked.

" 'Course not. I liked Sally when we were much younger—not like I like Vera though. You know that. She was real good company."

After a moment's silence Steve asked, "Do you reckon Vera'll come back? Have you heard from her?"

Hank stirred. The mention of Vera did something for him. "Yes, I've heard, had a note. Hope she'll be back soon. She's a Christian girl—believes like the Bible—" He spoke quietly as if informing himself.

The sound of a car motor interrupted the conversation of the boys. Both looked up. "I'd better go," Steve said, excusing himself. "It's your uncle Henry."

"Needn't hurry off. Can't imagine why he would be comin' here. He never does. Please don't leave now," Hank begged.

But Steve did hurry away, speaking to the man as he passed. Then, turning, he waved a good-bye to Hank.

By the time Hank got to the yard gate, his uncle had let himself out of his car and was leaning against the gatepost. The older man greeted his nephew with a smile that Hank thought looked sheepish.

"This is quite a surprise." Hank spoke, then wondered if he might have found better words to welcome his uncle. "Come right in," he tried again. "I'll call—"

The older man raised his hand in objection. "No, no, Son," he urged. "I—well—I really want to talk to you."

"To me? Sure, come on in," Hank invited again. "And we'll—"

Again Uncle Henry objected. "Just come to my automobile. We might even ride a little." A proud smile appeared on his face. "Like my Pierce-Arrow?"

Soon the two were spinning along the country road viewing the scenery on either side. If only the relationship between Henry Malcolm and his brother's son could have been as contented and serene, the two could have enjoyed the ride together fully.

"Hope I didn't cause your friend to leave," Uncle Henry apologized. "Believe he's a son of Mr. Worth," he commented. Then he cleared his throat. "Ahem! fine family—the Worths."

Hank wondered what his uncle might think of his poor kin rating friendship with the son of one of the wealthiest families in that part of the country.

The two Malcolms, closely related, yet so apart in

their relationship, rode quite some distance. The older man made bits of conversation now and then, while the other kept wondering what had brought about this particular ride. The Pierce-Arrow took one road and then turned on a cross path, going in another direction. With Indian blood surging through his veins, though, Hank was not lost. Besides, he had roamed the roads and hills and valleys of all that country, and he knew every road and trail for miles around. "Guess I'll go this way," Mr. Malcolm voiced. Then he headed straight toward Maple Hill. Now, curiosity ran high for Hank. He had never visited in his uncle's home before, and Aunt Violet was almost a stranger to him. He hoped his uncle wasn't taking him to their home.

"Do you like farming?" Uncle Henry ventured.

"Don't know much about anythin' else. Yes, sir, I like it." Hank answered, not a bit ashamed to own up to it.

Entering the Maple Hill community, the Pierce-Arrow, shining and black, turned onto the road that led toward the Brooks and Korrel homes. Uncle Henry lived on the road across the field. When the car stopped, both the homes so familiar to Hank could be seen in the distance. And Hank's heart seemed to beat a little faster, and his thoughts turned to Vera. He wondered if she had returned home. How he hoped she had by now. But the sound of his uncle's voice took these thoughts away.

"Look out across this field," Henry Malcolm said. He waved his arms as if stretching over the level acres in front of them. "There is an eighty back of my house," the uncle explained. "How would you like to have half of that piece of land, Son?"

113

Hank was astounded. He couldn't buy that land, if that was what his uncle was getting at.

His uncle went on, "Half of the finest eighty I've got. How would you like to have it? I'm gettin' too old now to take care of so much land, and it'd make some young man a good plot."

Hank gulped. "That'd be fine, Uncle Henry. Pretty land, I'll say. And who wouldn't like to have it? But I couldn't buy any small amount of it—not now. No, sir. I can't buy the land, if you're tryin' to sell it to me."

Henry looked straight at his nephew. "Look here, my boy," he said. "Ahem! I ain't tryin' to sell you no land. Fact is, it—ahem—should be yours. I mean, you deserve a good piece of land."

"Is he tryin' to gimme land that shoulda been Pa's? Is he too coward to admit it, but still wants to do something about it? Hank stood listening.

Uncle Henry began again, "I guess, Hank, I am really indebted to your pa," he confessed. "And I've been wantin' a long time to offer this eighty to you and to Toby together. Since you are my namesake, I wanted to mention it to you first. I felt that if I done that, I might repay your pa for—" Then Uncle Henry hushed, but he began again, "Oh, I ain't done nothin'—nothin' but exercise my rights. I ain't in-debted to nobody. I—I mean—oh, well—do you want half this eighty acres?"

"Don't feel obligated to us." Hank tried to help. "You don't have to—"

"No doubt Tom's told you what I done—I mean Tom's accused me." Henry Malcolm's face reddened. "That's it. He's accused me."

"Pa ain't talked much to us about you, Uncle Henry."

"But he's talked. Tom and Valindy's both talked. People will talk. Even kin do it. No trust to put in 'em," the old man stormed, then turned and walked around. Then he came back to Hank.

"I'd, I'd—uh, like to give this eighty to you and Toby," Uncle Henry said, his voice calming a bit. "I want you and Toby to have some of my property, as I said awhile ago. Toby's married and should have a start, and you—well, have you any plans of marriage, yet?"

"Sort of," Hank answered.

"Who's the fortunate girl?" his uncle asked managing a faint smile.

"You mean, who's the victim?" Hank joked. "I do have some thoughts. No plans." Hank fidgeted a bit. "I want to marry Vera Korrel, if I can."

Hank had not expected that these last words would cause such an outburst, a literal explosion. At the mention of Vera Korrel's name the man turned around, walked a step away, and put on such a demonstration, and said such words, that Hank wished he could disappear. Uncle Henry's eyes went wild, he reddened, and his hair seemed to stand on end. He stamped his feet and turned in circles. Then he bellowed, "Have you lost your senses, boy?" Uncle Henry took off his hat and fanned his face, returning the hat to the side of his head. "No kin of mine is gonna marry one of them quacks and still stay related to me. No. Not by a long shot."

Hank was too courteous to say so; but he felt that if anyone had lost his senses, surely Uncle Henry could rightly be accused of doing so. As for staying related to Uncle Henry, he had never felt the first bit of relationship to Uncle Henry Malcolm, whose name he had borne these nigh onto twenty years.

The man kept raging. "I hate them people—I hate the sight of their place!" he stormed. "I wished they'd—" Let it be enough to say that before the maddened man reached for the hand crank to start the automobile motor, he said a number of unpleasant things.

Turning the crank, the man said, "I've a mind to let you walk home." And it looked as if Hank would have to walk, for the motor did not start readily. Actually, the young man who had ridden to Maple Hill in the Pierce-Arrow preferred to walk back home.

"Please let me help," Hank offered, stepping up near the car's front. "I'm sorry—"

"Don't tell me you're sorry about nothin'. Just shut up, and remember that I won't give you a foot of my land. Not a foot. Toby can have it, if he wants it. All of it, the whole eighty."

"It's quite all right," Hank ventured. Then, although he had been told to shut up, he felt urged to offer his assistance again to the man who still was having trouble getting the motor started.

"What do you know about crankin' automobiles? Drivin' mules is different, you know."

The motor sputtered a few times, then started jerkily. But when the two were riding toward Oak Valley, the engine got to going more smoothly. However, the trip back to Hank's home was anything but smooth for Hank, who still smarted from Henry Malcolm's words.

Big Changes

For a day or so after the ride with Uncle Henry, Hank went about the place acting as if he were dreaming. He missed his sister, Susan. He could talk things over with her if she were at home. He also missed having Toby around—missed him terribly since the trip in the Pierce-Arrow to Uncle Henry's eighty acres. He wanted to talk about that with Toby. He was very reluctant to talk about it with Pa and Ma, for he hated to tell them of his uncle's behavior.

When Pa and Ma were alone, they made discussions about Hank's ride with Tom's brother, since Hank had made only casual remarks about it to them. "Why don't he tell us more about it?" Pa queried.

"Reckon what you heerd at the barbershop that day we went to Benston—'twas about ten years ago—reckon that's why Henry come over to see Hank?" Ma wondered. "Reckon that's it? About the will? Why can't the boy talk about it?"

Pa had little to say. He grunted, "Could be—or, well—give Hank time," was what Pa said.

"He ain't got that girl, Vera Korrel, outten his mind, as far as that goes," Ma said. "Henry might be helpin' him to get hitched up with her. She lives close to Henry. Reckon Henry'd do that?"

"Henry might do suprisin' things. Might try to help Hank against our wills, if he knowed what we don't want. But how could Henry know what we don't want or what we want?" After a bit of silence Pa spoke again. "Can't see why Hank don't see they don't come no better'n Sally Boutwell—and Sally wouldn't be hard for Hank to get, though Steve's sorta courtin' her now."

Nothing the two said unriddled the matter of Hank's recent ride with Henry. Pa and Ma sat down to rest on the back porch.

Hank's intentions were to let his parents know what had happened, and he decided that waiting would not make it any easier. It was not a pleasant experience to relate; and furthermore, when they learned that his interest in Vera was the cause of his loss of the forty acres that Uncle Henry had been about to give him, perhaps they would take a firmer stand against the girl he would like to have in his life.

Tom stepped over to the washbasin. "I'll wash up," he said. "Time to come to dinner. And I'm ready to eat, effen I can—appetite's gone with worryin'."

Valinda started toward the kitchen to put the food on the table.

"Pa," young Hank started. "You'll be shocked with what I tell you. But you'll have to believe it. Of course you and Ma's wonderin' why Uncle Henry came over the other day, and I went off with 'im."

Pa had a cupped handful of water to wash his face, but he let the water spill on the floor. Ma's looks might be described as those of a child waiting to hear a ghost story. But neither said a word.

"You know that eighty acres right back of Uncle Henry's place?" Hank started.

118

"Oh, yes, Son, very well. That shoulda been mine when my pa died. I had to borrow money, though, to buy this, 'cause I didn't get what was to be mine."

"Let 'im go on," Ma urged, standing there in the kitchen doorway. "We've done forgot about Henry's deal. And we've got along without his actual help—just a loan."

Ignoring their comments, Hank went on. "That's where he took me the other day. And here's where you'll be shocked." Hank was talking with a bit more ease now that he had started. "He told me that he wanted to give the eighty acres to me and to Toby, because he was indebted to you, Pa."

Tom and Valinda just stared. Pa's mouth gaped. Ma dropped onto a chair outside the door. "And I reckon you accepted it!" Pa stated.

"I couldn't," Hank said, then explained, " 'cause Uncle Henry backed out hisself."

"Backed out! What for? What did he back out for?" Ma asked, not sounding the least bit happy.

The answer to this was not going to be easy. It might cause much resentment toward the girl involved. No doubt Vera would now be blamed for all that had gone wrong. But Hank had started. He would tell them the whole story, regardless. "Well, it was because I told 'im I wanted to marry Vera," he ventured. "Uncle Henry hates the Korrel family because they are Adventists. He wouldn't give the land to me because of Vera." Then, in an effort to turn their thoughts from Vera, and to another point, he hastened to speak on. "He said he wanted to pay a debt he owed you, Pa."

That did turn the trend from Vera. Ma's voice was a bit loud—too loud—now. "Pay the debt to you that he owed yer pa!" Ma's face turned white, then red.

Hank broke in. "He may give it to Toby."

But Valinda was not through. "He shoulda done that long 'fore this. Why can't he come face-to-face with your pa? Why can't he, Tom? The coward! And on top of that, he's backed out on the boy," she said. "He ain't to be trusted no way." Then she sympathized, "The poor critter."

"The dirty rascal," Pa uttered. " 'Course he may remember Toby."

"It's your brother, Tom," Ma reminded her man.

"Valindy Malcolm, I know who I'm kin to!" Pa snapped. Then, stepping closer to his wife, he placed a hand on her shoulder and said, tenderly, "You and our young uns—well, that's who I am the most kin to. 'Course he's my kin, and I'd not harm him a mite. But if he feels that way about Hank's affairs—if he's gonna be that stubborn," Pa spoke, "well, it just ain't none of his business. It ain't none of his business what our young uns does, nor who they marry. If Hank wants to marry that girl, that's his own business, it is!"

Two faces turned toward Pa. He spoke a little more. "If he wants to be an Advent, 'tis none of Henry's business—and nobody's business."

"What do you mean, Pa?" Ma asked, as if not being able to understand.

"Yes," Tom Malcolm said further, "if he wants to be like that girl and marry her, that's none of Henry's business—it's nobody's business." Because he kept repeating himself, it seemed very evident that he was quite serious about what he said. Hank was astonished.

"You mean it's nobody's business but mine and

yours," Ma objected. "It surely—"

Pa looked straight at Ma, then spoke again, "I mean it's nobody's business. Like I said, it ain't nobody's business but his own—his O-W-N!" he spelled.

This was not at all what Hank had expected. He choked, and tears showed in his eyes.

Ma had another word—different from when she first heard Hank's story. "If you feel that way about the girl—about Vera—I'm with your Pa. It is your own business, like he said. And, if you want her for a wife—and if she wants you—we'll go along with you. Furthermore, if you take her, you'd better take her religion too. It's the only way for a man and woman to live together. They got to be united. They just have to be united in every way."

"Amen!" Pa added, reverently.

Few words were exchanged at the table while the three ate the noon meal. While Ma cleared the table and washed the dishes, Pa went to the barn. Hank made his way to his room and lay, face down, across his bed. Warm tears spilled on the covers.

"The Holy Spirit musta spoke to Pa and Ma," Hank whispered.

Things simmered down somewhat the next day after the Malcolms were so riled about Uncle Henry. "I want Toby to know about this," Pa said to Hank. " 'Course Toby can't do nothin' about it if Henry don't offer it to him, but I jest want him to know about it." Then his father asked Hank if he would go over to Toby's and talk with him. Hank agreed but suggested that he felt confident that his uncle was quite determined to dispose of that eighty acres of land, for it seemed to be weighing on his mind, and surely he would tell Toby himself.

"There'll be a way for you too, Son, without that land Henry refused you. We've never depended on Henry for nothin'—nothin' but a loan that's been paid, and we ain't lookin' to him now. Me and Ma'll stand behind you."

That evening work at the Malcolm place was finished early, and Hank made ready to go to Toby's at his father's request. "Take a loaf of bread I baked today," Ma said. She handed the package to Hank as he walked out. "Nancy'll be proud of it, I know; and Toby'll eat several slices while it's fresh."

The shortcut made quick traveling between Hank's home and his brother's place. While walking with long strides, young Malcolm let his mind wander to the home only a short distance from Toby and Nancy's. Could Vera have come home yet? Could she still care for him, as he was confident she did before the day she had come to the field to tell him she was going away?

Stepping upon the wooden floor of the front porch where Toby and Nancy lived, Hank called, "Anybody home?"

The front door came open. "Here's your big brother," Nancy called to Toby. She welcomed Hank in. "I jest knowed you'd come tonight," she said, chuckling her delight to see him. "Set down. Toby'll be here in a minute." She set a pan of roasted peanuts on the hearth before Hank. "I parched these goobers today. Musta figured somehow that you'd come." Nancy took the loaf of bread to the kitchen, talking as she went. *"Somebody's home!"* she notified her brother-in-law, smiling and winking at him. But the words fell on deaf ears, for Hank did not hear that. Had he heard, it would have sounded more like refreshing music than mere words.

Toby joined his brother. "A little cool since the sun set. Made a fire." That was Toby's greeting. "Reckon old man winter'll be payin' us a visit before many days."

Hank thought he would mention about the land right away, but he didn't have to. From the kitchen came Nancy's voice. "Guess what we got today?" she asked. She came in then to sit with Hank and Toby.

"Couldn't guess in years," was Hank's answer, though he thought perhaps he could.

Toby pulled a long folded piece of paper from the table close by and held it up for his brother to see.

"A land deed?" Hank asked, because he thought he knew.

"Yep! And the ink's hardly dry that was used to sign the names that made eighty acres of land mine—mine and Nancy's!" Toby boasted, unfolding the deed and showing the paper. "See. 'Henry Malcolm' on the first line, and below his name is 'Violet Malcolm.' That was written today."

"We could hardly believe it," Nancy said. "Reckon why he done that? Reckon he means it for a weddin' present? But we're mighty proud of it, anyway."

"That's what I come over to tell you—I mean to ask you about," Hank stammered.

"Then you knowed about it?" questioned Nancy, saucily.

"How'd you know?" Toby questioned.

"Well," Hank told them, "you see Uncle Henry come to see me and said he wanted to give us both the land—"

"So you've come to get your half?" Nancy snapped.

"Quiet down, wifey," Toby commanded.

"Indeed not," Hank assured them. "He offered—"

"The buzzard," Nancy called the man who had just made her and Toby owners of a fine piece of land. "You first." Then she asked, "Why didn't you take it?"

"Because he refused to give it to me because of Vera. He—"

But Hank was cut off again. "Serves you right," Nancy came back. "Why let folks like her come between you and half a fine piece of land?"

"She's your friend," her husband of only a few months told her.

"Some things are more valuable than land," Hank said kindly.

"Like what?" Nancy asked.

Seeing the evening would not be very pleasant— just confusion—Hank made it convenient to leave early.

"No need to rush off. We ain't mad." Nancy begged.

With a forced smile, Hank closed the door between him and the brother who had been so close to him. He would wait for the heated feelings of his sister-in-law to cool.

The moon shone crystal clear, but now and then a cloud overshadowed it. As Hank, twice hurt about a piece of land, moved onto the path to go toward Oak Valley, he became aware of someone coming toward him. It was the figure of a woman, he thought. Then the lonely young man had a hunch that made his heart skip a beat.

Joy at Last

Having left his brother's house, Hank moved out onto the path with a heavy heart. However, he was approaching the someone who had brought about suspicion, and something inside him wanted to be glad. Closer they came to each other, until Hank's suspicions turned into reality. "It's you, Vera!" he exclaimed. "It's *you*!" His voice was full of happiness. "I had wondered when you'd be home. Now you're back."

By the time Hank had finished all those words, he had reached the girl. In the moonlight she looked lovely to him. He took her by the arm and turned her around to walk with him to a rail fence, where they stopped to talk. "Were you goin' to Nancy's?" he asked.

"I was going to offer my congratulations to the newlyweds." Vera smiled. "Mama and Jasper told me about it—about the wedding. It must have been rather cute the way they were married. Papa spoke of it too."

Although the evening was lovely, the night air was cool. Hank reached out and pulled Vera's jacket to bring it snugly together under her chin. But when she protested, Hank thought her protest to be from indifference. "Not again!" he said right out loud. But how could Vera know that he referred to the many jolts that had come to him since she had been away? Hank spoke hurriedly. "Don't you care anymore? Or, did you ever? Do your folks—?"

Vera interrupted his last words, speaking words of her own that she had never voiced to Hank. "Perhaps my folks would oppose our friendship if—well, if they knew we liked each other." Her eyes moistened. Hank wondered if she was also having a struggle. Vera talked on, "It's not because it's you that they would oppose. They like you a lot. But it's my faith— or your lack of it," she said frankly. "It's *that* that makes the difference. But I had to make the decision myself. Hank," the girl spoke with hesitancy, "I cannot become 'unequally yoked' with you. I cannot be 'unequally yoked' with anyone." The girl did not hide her tears. She seemed embarrassed.

Hank understood now. Now he would tell her all. He pulled her close to him, though she resisted still. Maybe now her struggle and his could be over. It took only minutes for him to tell her about his experience the day he rode to Maple Hill in his uncle's car. Then he told her of his parents' opposition. But, with happiness showing in his face, he told her of his own Christian experience—his conflict of mind—since he had known her and especially since he had attended the meetings at the big tent. He told her that he had made his decision to follow his Lord and Saviour. And, he added, "My parents have changed their attitude toward you and have told me that they would not even oppose me if I, myself, wanted to be an Adventist. And I know it's the right thing to do."

Vera looked absolutely amazed. There were seconds of silence. When she seemed to pull herself together, she asked, "Do you mean all this, Hank? Do you really mean it?" Tears welled up but did not spill over. The girl went on, "You aren't trying to—?"

"I wouldn't lie to you, Vera," Hank assured her. "Even if I can't have you."

"Then you mean—"

"Of course I do. Every word. I never went to church much until I knew you. I never had much thought about God. Now, it is the joy of my life. I intend to be a Christian, even if I have to be one without you. I hope, though, we can live the life together. Not for ourselves only, but to help others too—maybe my own folks."

"It's a big step to take. So different, and there will be trials in the path—mountains to surmount," Vera said, her head resting on Hank's shoulder.

"That I know. That will make the kingdom all the more precious." Hank spoke, unaccustomed to this kind of talk. "But I have made my decision, and I intend to be a Seventh-day Adventist."

"For this I have prayed, Hank."

"How can I meet the temptations?" Hank queried.

"It is true temptations will come. Jesus says, though, 'Lo, I am with you alway' and that is the comfort we can have. He promises us rest unto our souls."

"I'll depend on that," Hank answered. "And I'll have you as my helpmate, won't I?"

Vera nodded. Looking up at Hank she added, "Jesus never fails."

"And He will not fail me," the new Christian spoke with confidence. "I have found two great joys, Vera— the joy of finding Jesus, and the joy of finding you."

The ears of the young couple did not hear the noisy

night creatures making their love music. But, as the whippoorwill called to its mate, and as the crickets chirped in the thicket, the happiest moment that could come to two young people had now come to Hank and Vera.

And so it was on Pa's farm. Vera and Hank joined their lives and their dreams of the future, and their dedicated exemplary Christian lives did much to influence those remaining on and around Pa's farm.